KU-203-521

MYSTERY AT BLACK BOULDER

Ex-army scout Lance Costigan was deputed to act as a detective on the Indian reservation. His mission was to prevent a Sioux uprising, fuelled by renegades selling them rifles and firewater. So it was that Lance rode into Black Boulder to confront Eben Shaintuck, a notorious gunrunner. But there were also two other men menacingly armed with six-guns. Even if Lance could survive this encounter, his job would only just have begun and it would be a long, hard struggle before the threat of violence was over.

DC HE

Allington Library
Castle Road
Allington
Kent ME16 0UP
01622 683435

MAI

04 DEC 2018

3 |9|,9

HE

21.

29. JAN 09   2 3 JUN 2009   1 1 AUG 2021

7 MAR 08   2 4 OCT 2009

04. JUN 08   − 2 MAR 2011

2 3 JUL 2011

2 5 OCT 2018

Books should be returned or renewed by the
last date stamped above

_____

_____

_____

Awarded for excellence

C152761934

SPECIAL MESSAGE TO READERS

This book is published under the auspices of

THE ULVERSCROFT FOUNDATION

(registered charity No. 264873 UK)

Established in 1972 to provide funds for research, diagnosis and treatment of eye diseases. Examples of contributions made are: —

A Children's Assessment Unit at Moorfield's Hospital, London.

•

Twin operating theatres at the Western Ophthalmic Hospital, London.

•

A Chair of Ophthalmology at the Royal Australian College of Ophthalmologists.

•

The Ulverscroft Children's Eye Unit at the Great Ormond Street Hospital For Sick Children, London.

You can help further the work of the Foundation by making a donation or leaving a legacy. Every contribution, no matter how small, is received with gratitude. Please write for details to:

**THE ULVERSCROFT FOUNDATION,
The Green, Bradgate Road, Anstey,
Leicester LE7 7FU, England.
Telephone: (0116) 236 4325**

**In Australia write to:
THE ULVERSCROFT FOUNDATION,
c/o The Royal Australian and New Zealand
College of Ophthalmologists,
94-98, Chalmers Street, Surry Hills,
N.S.W. 2010, Australia**

ROBERT J. MARTELL

MYSTERY AT BLACK BOULDER

Complete and Unabridged

LINFORD
Leicester

First hardcover published in 2003
by Robert Hale Limited, London
Originally published in paperback as
Red Man's Territory by Robert J. Martell

First Linford Edition
published 2005
by arrangement with
Robert Hale Limited, London

The moral right of the author has been asserted

All characters in this books are fictitious and
any resemblance to any real person or
circumstance is unintentional.

Copyright © 1957, 2003 by A. A. Glynn
All rights reserved

British Library CIP Data

Martell, Robert J., *1929* –
    Mystery at Black Boulder.—Large print ed.—
    Linford western library
    1. Western stories 2. Large type books
    I. Title II. Martell, Robert J., *1929* – .
    Red man's territory
    823.9'14 [F]

    ISBN 1–84395–774–4

KENT
ARTS & LIBRARIES

C\ 52761934

Published by
F. A. Thorpe (Publishing)
Anstey, Leicestershire

Set by Words & Graphics Ltd.
Anstey, Leicestershire
Printed and bound in Great Britain by
T. J. International Ltd., Padstow, Cornwall

This book is printed on acid-free paper

1

A raw wind whipped out of the badlands and went keening icily over the bleak plains, foreboding, like the threat of coming tragedy. It whistled about the buildings of Black Boulder, a settlement of clustered shacks which rose abruptly from the prairie, stirring up billows of gritty dust and whirling scatterings of litter about the town's single street, now shrouded by early evening.

Through the swirls of eye-stinging dust, walking with his head held well down, came a man. He was tall and as lean as whipcord, garbed in the usual rig of a plains cowboy but lacking the broad leather chaps at his legs. Yellow lamplight, blooming from the windows of Black Boulder's stores, highlighted his passing form momentarily and picked out the single Colt .45 buckled at his right thigh.

Where the false-fronted bulk of the Dakota Palace Hotel reared upwards, half-a-dozen saddled cowponies stood hitched, turning their rumps into the cutting blast of the wind. The tall man paused for an instant to survey the huddled animals, as though looking for a particular horse, then he swivelled on his heel, mounted the gallery of the saloon-cum-hotel and entered. Inside, a scattering of cow-wranglers and two or three blue uniformed soldiers, off duty, stood at the bar where a stout barkeep with a bald head and scrubby beard presided. The newcomer paused just inside the door, casting dark eyes over the drinkers who, in turn, studied him. They saw a lean, copper-coloured face with a high-bridged nose and coal-black eyes regarding them from under the wide brim of a high-crowned stetson. His cheekbones, sharp nose and jet hair, worn longer than was fashionable at this period, gave an indication of the strong strain of Indian blood in the tall newcomer.

His sloe eyes fastened on a grizzled old-timer standing with two range-garbed men. All three looked obvious saddle-tramps. The grizzled oldster passed a nervous hand across his chin when he saw the newcomer watching him. The slightest quirk touched the lips of the tall man and he strode purposefully towards the oldster.

'You're Eben Shaintuck,' he said without any preliminary. It was a statement, not a question.

'Yeah,' drawled the oldster, his voice whiskey-thickened.

'Do you know who I am?' The dark, Indian eyes were boring into those of the old-timer.

'Sure, you're Lance Costigan, the son of Malachy Costigan who was a scout for the army in the old days. I've seen you around — you ride range somewhere in these parts.'

'Not any more,' replied Lance Costigan quietly. 'I don't ride range any more. What do you know about the reservation Sioux gettin' whiskey an' rifles?' The question was a whip-crack.

'Me? What would I know about it?' The oldster's voice had a high edge of injured innocence. His saddle-tramp companions shuffled uneasily.

'Listen, Shaintuck, I'm not given to mixin' words none. The ghost dance craze is spreading among the Sioux, there's big trouble on the way an' certain whites are sellin' rifles an' firewater to the Indians. I'm lookin' for the men who are dealin' in booze an' guns — lookin' for them on the sayso of the United States Government an' the authorities at Standing Rock Indian Agency — '

'What you askin' me about it for?' cut in Eben Shaintuck, still maintaining his attitude of injured innocence. 'Why should you look me up an' ask me about booze — an' gun-runnin'?'

Shaintuck's younger partners were displaying an uneasiness which showed them to be on the thin edge of grabbing for their guns. Costigan watched them from the corner of a calculating black eye. He answered Shaintuck's question, speaking slowly:

'Because it's whispered that you were in on the gun-runnin' game back in '76. Rumours have it you were one of the *hombres* who supplied the Sioux with rifles they used to massacre Custer's Seventh Cavalry at the Little Big Horn. What you did fourteen years ago, you might do again!'

Eben Shaintuck glowered at Lance Costigan with wicked little eyes.

'You can't prove that!' he hissed. 'Ain't nobody can prove that — you have nothin' to go on, Costigan!'

'It's plumb peculiar that you an' your sidekicks should show up around the reservation territory just when the Sioux are half-crazed with their new-fangled ghost dancin' routine an' ready to give their ears for guns.'

One of the old-timer's partners pushed his way forward. He was a tall youngster dressed in scuffed jeans and wearing a heavy yellow slicker against the raw weather of these early December days. Under the greasy brim of his big sombrero, his face was tight-lipped and lantern-jawed. He held his hands on his hips and his slicker was pulled back to reveal a Colt .44 holstered low. Lance Costigan noted that, as well as a cartridge-studded gun-belt, he wore a waist-belt with a buckle on which the initials CSA were raised. It was an old Confederate Army buckle, a thirty-year-old relic the man had picked up somewhere, for he was too young to have fought in the Civil War. He pushed himself forward with an insolent smirk on his thin face. Lance could smell the whiskey on his breath when he spoke.

'Who the hell are you to come questionin' white men? A damn half-breed! Your old man was a squaw-lover an' your mother was a full-blooded Sioux — '

The insult was not completed. With a swift movement Lance Costigan grabbed the speaker's slicker with his left hand, pulled the man towards him and looped a rock-hard bunch of range-toughened knuckles upwards to crack a forceful blow across the beard-stubbled jaw. The youngster flopped backwards in a loose heap.

Costigan whirled about in time to intercept the second of Shaintuck's companions who was in the act of grabbing his holstered six-gun. Wading in with his head low, Costigan drove a savage blow into the fellow's ribs to send him spinning back on his heels, robbed of his wind. Lance followed up, hooking a cracking blow to the gunny's chin, sending him to the floor to join his dazed partner. Anticipating trouble from Shaintuck, Costigan swung round to face the oldster. He found him with his hand already moving towards the black butt of the revolver holstered at his belt. The half-breed's right hand streaked down and up in an eye-defying arc. His forty-five had cleared leather before Shaintuck's gnarled fingers completed their grip around the butt of his weapon.

'Don't give me any excuse to kill you, Shaintuck,' breathed Lance, covering the grizzled old man squarely. Shaintuck's hand dropped helplessly away from his gun-butt.

Costigan jerked his head towards Shaintuck's companions now gathering themselves up dazedly from the scuffed floor.

'Get your friends out of here — an' keep away from the reservations with your lousy rot-gut in future. I have no proof about you bein' involved in gun-runnin', but I do know you sold whiskey to a pair of Chief Running Pony's bucks only this afternoon. Your kind are no good to whites and Indians alike, so clear out of this country while you still have a whole hide. That goes for the three of you!!'

Shaintuck's young companions, both winded, staggered across to the old-timer, who was glowering wickedly at Lance Costigan. The half-breed kept them covered while the trio made for the door, bestowing malevolent backward glances on the copper-skinned young man who held the mouth of his Colt unwaveringly upon them.

When the batwing doors of the saloon had closed upon the departing backs of the three men, the tension that had gripped the bar-room when the violence started was relaxed. The men at the bar, who had swung about and fanned out to watch the brief fight, bundled themselves together in groups once more and resumed the serious business of drinking. One of them, however, a Cavalry sergeant, left the bar and crossed to where Lance Costigan stood holstering his six-gun.

'Nice way you handled those *hombres*, Lance,' observed the sergeant, who was a tanned-featured, grey-haired veteran. 'That Shaintuck don't look like much, but he's pizen. I came across him in the Sioux and Apache campaigns of the '70s. He was runnin' guns, all right, but no one could prove it.'

'It's my guess he's turned up in this territory for the same purpose,' Costigan replied, moving towards the bar. 'I know he's started dabbling in whiskey trading because I found two of Running Pony's braves hopelessly drunk on the reservation this afternoon. They told me they bought the firewater from an old white man and two younger ones. They were too stupid with booze to describe the men, but I got it out of one that the oldster rode a dappled mare. I knew Shaintuck had been seen around Black Boulder on that kind of cayuse so I came lookin' for him an' spotted the mare hitched outside.' Lance signalled to the bartender for two drinks to be set up. 'How're things back at Fort Yates, Zeb?' he asked the non-com.

'Kinda panicky under the surface of ordinary routines. It's always that way when there's Indian trouble expected,' answered Sergeant Zeb Dockery. The old campaigner had been a particular friend of Lance's father, the army scout, Malachy Costigan, and had known Lance since he was a youngster trailing about the army settlements of the frontier with his hard-bitten father.

Old Malachy Costigan had met his end during the campaign against Cochise and his Arizona Apaches some years before. His son had spent some time as a military scout but, of later years, with the comparative settlement of the frontier, had taken to cow-punching with a Dakota outfit. When the fantastic outbreak of 'ghost-dancing' had spread to the Sioux and the medicine-men were predicting that the Great Spirit was about to punish all whites and return the land to the tribes, the half-breed, with his knowledge of Sioux ways, had been commissioned by the army to act as a detective on the reservations of that people.

'No tellin' how this craze will finish up, Zeb,' he said as he and the sergeant drank at the bar. 'The majority of settlements on Standing Rock reservation have been affected. The Indians have been dancin' themselves into a fury every day with the medicine-men whippin' them up, or promisin' them that the so-called magic shirts they're wearing are proof against the white soldiers' bullets an' that the day of the whites is comin' to a close.'

'Dancin' don't do them no harm, I guess,' remarked Zeb Dockery. 'That won't do nothin' but make 'em tired. I hate to think what would happen if they get whiskey an' guns while they're in this crazy religious mood an' some fool medicine-man gives the war-path signal.'

'Whiskey an' guns are what the army is concerned about, Zeb. One or two malcontent whites like Shaintuck an' his sidekicks have shown up lately. They'll bear watchin', but General Miles has a notion that there's a big brain at work behind the booze an' gun-smugglin'. The amount of whiskey and guns you army boys found on the Pine Ridge reservation last month showed that the stuff got in on a big scale an' the traffic was well organised. I'm inclined to agree with the general that the whole business is more than two-cent smugglin' carried out by one or two bad whites.'

'Sure is funny how you get would-be gun-runners showin' up when the threat of an Indian risin' is in the air,' the sergeant said. 'I saw the same breed at work in the earlier Sioux troubles an' the Apache risin's in the Southwest — them bad whites must have a down on their own kind!'

The non-commissioned officer ordered two more drinks.

'They got plenty of scope for sellin' guns to the tribes while this ghost-dance mania has a hold on them,' he added.

'Sure, if we don't root 'em out quick,' replied Lance Costigan grimly.

'How're things over at Spring River reservation?' queried Zeb Dockery.

'Last time I was there things were quiet, Chief White Buffalo was holdin' his people in check. He wasn't havin' any part of the ghost-dance stuff. He regarded it as one of Sittin' Bull's moves an' he has no love for Sittin' Bull. I'm takin' a room here tonight, an' headin' over toward Spring River tomorrow to take a look-see if White

Buffalo is still holdin' off the outbreaks of dancin'.'

'That agent over at Spring River, Joe Folinsbee, what sort of galoot is he?' Dockery asked. 'I seen him around Fort Yates a couple of times when he came in to report to the colonel. Strikes me as a plumb greasy *hombre*.'

'He's a run-of-the-mill Indian agent,' Costigan replied, without enthusiasm. 'Maybe he's not such a strong-handed an' efficient man as Jim McLaughlin over at Standing Rock, but I guess he manages all right — especially since he's backed up by wise old Chief White Buffalo.'

Costigan had no idea why Dockery had been prompted to ask such a question about Joe Folinsbee, but it had touched an edge of doubt that had been niggling at his mind since he had been riding the Sioux reservations on behalf of the military authorities. There was something about Agent Folinsbee that set Costigan to wondering how far the agent could be trusted. It was nothing

14

definite, nothing the half-breed could grasp at, but there was something in the oily Folinsbee that reminded Lance of the old-time, grafting Indian agents, who had not all been weeded out by the clean-up of the Indian traders in the middle '70s. Apparently, that same indefinite doubt had rankled shrewd old Zeb Dockery, too.

Even after he had wished the old soldier a good night and settled down in the room he had booked at the Dakota Palace, Lance found no rest from this rankling doubt.

'Funny,' he mused as he lay in bed, 'that Zeb should have the same feelin' about Folinsbee!'

He lay listening to the sound of the wind whining around the clapboard hotel for some time before sleep claimed him. In the keening and whistling, he fancied he heard the names of Folinsbee and Shaintuck constantly outside the window of the room, while the distant thunder of war-drums and Sioux war-yelps sounded in the background.

2

The following morning broke cold with the threat of snow contained in the heavy walls of leaden cloud that clustered over the plains. The ice-edged wind was still keening in off the rolling land, raking the street of Black Boulder, when Lance Costigan, shaved and breakfasted, made his way from the Dakota Palace to the livery-stable where he had left his bay gelding the previous night.

Costigan saddled his mount and struck off in a westward direction for the reservation at Spring River. Soon, the township of Black Boulder was lost beyond a fold of the plain at his back, and he was riding at a steady walk over the frost-crisped ground. He was a big, bulky figure in the saddle, looking top-heavy in the heavy-quilted slicker so necessary to a prairie rider in the

North-Western winter. Lance Costigan thought deeply as he rode.

Through his mind ran the outline of events which had stirred up the threat of an Indian uprising in this winter of 1890. A chain of disturbing and fanatical activities which had dragged on for more than a year and was now coming to a head.

The previous year, wily old Sitting Bull, one-time war chief, medicine-man and hater of the whites, heard of the dreams of one Wovoka, an Indian in Nevada. This Wovoka, it seemed, had been entrusted by the Great Spirit with the means of driving the white man from the Indian hunting grounds. Sitting Bull, who was living a quiet and apparently settled life on the Standing Rock reservation, sent a messenger, one Kicking Bear, to inquire into the message of Wovoka.

Kicking Bear returned with a fantastic story which found ready credence among the reservation Sioux. The main burden of the story was that the reign of the white man was coming to an end. The whites had stolen the land from the Indian; killed the buffalo which had fulfilled almost all the material needs of the red-men; herded the Indians into reservations and, since the disastrous winter of 1886–87, had cut down the beef ration of the reservation Indians almost to starvation point. But it was all about to end. The Great Spirit had said so — through Wovoka, his prophet!

Wovoka said the Great Spirit had revealed to him that the land would be renewed with fresh soil to a level five times higher than a man. All the white men would be buried under this new, fertile land which would run with new rivers and provide grazing for renewed herds of bison. The day of the whites would be over, for the Great Spirit would miraculously close all land and water routes into the Indian lands. The Great Spirit would cause the guns of the whites to have no effect upon the red-men for, if the Indians went into battle wearing shirts, these would be rendered bullet-proof.

Such was the revelation Kicking Bear brought to Sitting Bull. But the day of triumph was not to come without rigorous preparation. The Indians must prepare for the coming of the ghosts who were to reveal the time of action, they must not cause trouble but dance the strenuous 'ghost-dance' daily until the Great Spirit sent his ghostly messengers from the world of spirits.

So it went on through 1889, the Indians dancing the frenzied ghost-dance daily, working themselves into a half-mad ecstasy until many fell exhausted. Throughout the reservations of the North-West, the Sioux tribes were dancing, the wily medicine-men were whipping the tribes into a fanatical fury, and the land reverberated with the stamp of moccasins and the wild whooping and chanting of the ghost-songs.

'It's a craze an' it'll die out,' opined some whites.

'It'll lead to a Sioux uprising an' we'll

all be wiped out!' contradicted others. And so it went on, month following panicky month. The whites, who had begun to think of the frontier as almost settled found themselves living under the threat of a savage uprising. Some began to clamour for military protection and, in November 1889, President Benjamin Harrison ordered troops to the Dakotas. The dancing continued, frenzied, but still without violence toward the whites. The soldiers watched and waited.

Into the panic-edged state of affairs came the threat of gun-running. Bad whites were seen drifting about close to the reservations and the discovery of modern Winchesters cached on land in the Pine Ridge Agency proved to the authorities that a shrewd eye was needed to watch the reservations. The military had sent for Lance Costigan, son of the famed old Indian scout, a man who was trusted by the Sioux, one who had loyalties to both white and red men and one with an unrelenting hatred for the 'bad white' element who sold guns and whiskey to the Indians.

'Ride the reservations,' Costigan had been ordered. 'Keep your eyes open for booze and gun-trading. Whiskey and guns — the matches which could explode the keg of gunpowder and turn the fanatical, ghost-dancing Sioux into a murdering horde on the war-path.'

Although the ghost-dance crisis worried Lance Costigan and he had a niggling worry about Agent Folinsbee — which had been brought to the surface of his mind when Sergeant Zeb Dockery mentioned the Indian agent's name out of the blue the previous evening — he found an exquisite pleasure in riding towards the Spring River reservation. Eloise would be there.

In the Sioux dialect, her name meant Sun-on-Water and she was the daughter of Lance's friend, Chief White Buffalo. Like Lance, she belonged to two worlds, that of the red man and the white. Although she had spent some

21

time in St Paul, where she had been educated in white ways and the name Eloise had been bestowed on her, she had returned to her father and the Indian life she loved. This life was only a shadow of what it had been before the red man was herded on to the reservation lands, but Eloise Sun-on-Water could not live away from sun, sky and wind. So she had returned to her people, the proud red people to whom the whites smugly referred as 'savage'.

Before the riding man, the wide, wind-raked plain rolled away to where the gnarled peaks of the badlands reared up against the leaden sky. Away to Costigan's left, a straggling outcrop of the badland structure formed a wall of tumbled boulders some fifty feet high. Costigan was riding close to the outcropping for it served to break the cutting wind.

'*Crack! Whang!*'

The bark of a Winchester came clattering flatly out of the rugged cluster of boulders. Costigan felt his hat snatched from his head as the whining bullet ripped into it close to the crown. Lance threw himself low in the saddle, hugging his bare head into the offside of the gelding's neck. As he did so, he caught sight of a white puff of smoke drifting off the face of the huddle of boulders.

Lance slipped the Colt from his holster and spurred the horse in towards the base of the outcropping in one swift action.

The man on the outcropping fired again, the Winchester's roar shattering the crisp winter air. The moving target baffled the sniper, but the slug whizzed uncomfortably close to Costigan's ear for all that.

The mounted man, canted low in his saddle, clattered into the loose scree at the foot of the rocky outcrop. He swung down from the gelding and crouched behind a sun-split rock, Colt cocked. He edged around the rock and surveyed the rugged face of the outcrop, but could see no sign of the Winchester-artist concealed up there. Costigan ensured that the reins of his horse were thrown over the animal's head to rest against its knees — the cattleman's simple but effective method of preventing a horse from wandering — then he began to creep along the base of the outcrop, half doubled up. The man up in the boulders saw him moving among the scree and fired again. The crash of the weapon and the screech of the bullet shattered the silence of the brooding cluster of rocks. Costigan threw himself flat on the ground as the slug whizzed over his head like an angry leaden hornet. He rolled for the safety of a big boulder and, in doing so, caught sight of a yellow slicker showing itself from among the clusters of loose rock high on the face of the outcroppings. The wintry sun put a hard sheen on the barrel of a Winchester and the fellow fired again.

Lance cursed as the bullet whanged off the rock which sheltered him. The sniper had his position marked and the rock was in full range of the rifleman. The half-breed had put himself in a position in which he could easily be pinned down by the rifleman in the high rocks of the outcrop.

He waited through a silent and panic-edged minute and thumbed a slug from his belt-loops into the empty chamber of his six-gun. Then, he showed himself cautiously around the edge of the sheltering rock, revolver ready. He chose exactly the right moment, for the rifleman upon the rock face had also moved out of cover and was in the act of surveying Costigan's position. He was a big-hatted, yellow-slickered figure, but the details of his face were distance-blurred. He jumped back in surprise as Lance showed himself and began to level the Winchester, but Costigan was quicker and triggered a couple of quick shots at the figure on the rock face.

The rewarding sound of a yelp of pain sounded as he edged back into cover and he had a brief glimpse of the rifleman staggering back, the Winchester falling from his grip. From up in the high rocks of the rugged outcrop, he heard a metallic clattering and shoved his nose out of cover inquisitively. He saw the gleam of the Winchester falling down the tumbled scree and skittering off the hard rocks.

'So the guy's lost his rifle,' he thought with satisfaction. 'That evens the odds a little, anyway!'

He snapped out of rumination at once with the realisation that Yellow Slicker was running for it, dodging from rock to rock. As he came into momentary view, Costigan saw that he was clutching his left side.

Lance held his position and waited until the running figure again appeared in the gap between two large rocks up on the scree. He fired on the running, wounded man without remorse — for the fleeing Yellow Slicker had, after all, attempted to 'dry gulch' him. The bullet from the Colt merely snatched at the running man's wide-brimmed hat before he disappeared behind another boulder.

Lance Costigan cursed the difficulty of hitting accurately with a Colt at this range. He waited, watching a gnarled rocky cluster behind which the running man seemed to have disappeared. He could hear a brief and distant scuffling, as of loose scree being disturbed by slithering boots. Then, silence and no further sign of the fleeing, would-be bush-whacker.

Costigan realised that there must be some quick way down from the heights of the outcropping and he began to run through the tangled groups of rocks at its base as fast as he could.

The sudden, muffled *clump* of unshod hoofs sounded up ahead of him as he dodged from behind a rock and he saw Yellow Slicker, mounted on a piebald mustang, break out of the rock clusters about two hundred yards ahead of him, hightailing for the open land.

'Ridin' an Indian pony!' thought Costigan as he slammed a shot after the speeding rider. The sturdy mustang was making good speed and Lance's bullet whanged away into the rocks harm-lessly.

The half-breed spat out a cowboy cuss-word. His own horse was too far back in the rocks for him to give chase and, even if he had the gelding close to hand, he knew there was little hope of outstripping the speedy Indian pony. Disgustedly, he watched the scanty plume of dust, risen from the frost-packed ground by the running pony, growing smaller as the yellow-slickered rider split the wind in the general direction of Black Boulder.

'Who in tarnation was he?' Lance asked himself, half-aloud as he trekked back among the rocks in search of his hat. The garb of the mysterious rifleman was no guide to his identity. Almost everybody out here wore a yellow slicker and a broad-brimmed sombrero in the winter.

'Ridin' an Indian pony!' repeated the half-breed. 'Where'd he get that critter — 'less he was at the Spring River reservation?' He made his way back to where the bay gelding was waiting patiently, nuzzling among the barren rocks in a futile search for grazing. He remembered the fact that the man who had tried to kill him had dropped his Winchester when Costigan had winged him. After some minutes of searching amid the scatterings of scree, he found the rifle.

It was an ordinary, well-oiled '73 model without initials carved on the butt or any other marking to provide a clue to ownership. Carrying the Winchester, he climbed the outcrop to the place from where the man had first fired on him.

The point where the sniper had originally been holed up was a rocky ledge behind the shelter of a rock. The ledge was carpeted with a spread of loose sand. Indian reasoning set to work in Lance's mind: a man lying here would have a good chance of hitting another riding on the plain. The man in the yellow slicker must have been no great marksman to merely pluck at his hat when throwing a Winchester slug from this vantage point.

'*A man lying here!*' yipped an excited voice in the half-breed's mind and his heart gave a leap as he saw a peculiar depression marked in the loose sand of the ledge. Blurred in the sand, but quite unmistakable, were the imprints of three letters in reverse — CSA. The marks that would be left by the raised letters of an old Confederate States Army belt-buckle if a man wearing such a buckle had lain here on the sandy ledge.

'So he left his brand in his back-trail,' murmured Lance. 'An' he's Eben Shaintuck's sidekick — the fellow I slugged in the Dakota Palace last night! His slicker was open just enough to allow the buckle of his belt to print itself into the sand!'

Lance walked down the tumbled, loose scree towards his bay gelding, wondering about the attempt to kill him made by the youngster who strung along with Shaintuck.

The fellow could not have holed up

in the rocks on the off-chance that Costigan would come that way. The only man to whom Lance had confided his intention of riding to Spring River was Sergeant Zeb Dockery and the man with the rebel belt-buckle had not been in the bar-room of the hotel at the time.

Then there was the puzzling business of the mustang. The man had been riding an Indian pony — saddled, he had noted.

Lance mounted his horse and resumed riding in the direction of the Spring River reservation. Ruminating as he rode, he decided that Shaintuck's partner must have been riding close to the rocky outcrop, saw and recognised him as he approached and holed himself up in the rocks to snipe at him, possibly motivated by revenge for the swipe Costigan took at him the previous night.

Or was he motivated by something deeper? Had he been to the reservation at Spring River on some shady business in which guns and liquor figured? And why had he been mounted on an Indian mustang?

Chewing on these rankling questions, Lance rode for an hour until the rough wooden administrative buildings of the Spring River Agency came into view. The commissary store, where the reservation Indians gathered for their monthly rations, the shack that served as Agent Folinsbee's office and living quarters, the clutter of small buildings and the peeled pole corrals were huddled in a fold in the plain.

In front of the agent's office there was a cluster of blanketed figures and Lance wondered why so many of the Sioux should be at the agency head-quarters at that time; it was not ration day. He caught sight of Agent Joe Folinsbee and two or three of his white helpers moving excitedly among the Indians and, as he rode into earshot, he became aware of a mournful dirge being chanted in high, feminine voices.

Something leaped coldly inside him at the thought that old White Buffalo had lost his grip on his people and the ghost-dance mania had broken out among them. Then he caught the words of the Sioux dirge and realised that it was not a ghost-dance chant, but a death-song, chanted by a line of blanketed squaws sitting against the wooden wall of the store.

He rode into the knot of Indians, who parted silently at his coming, and saw that they were clustering about the still form of a young brave who lay on the frost-hardened ground with glassy eyes wide open in death.

3

The wide Missouri River and miles of rolling plains separated the Spring River Agency and the town of Bismarck. In those two locations, at the same moment on that winter-edged morning, two men were faced with their own particular problems. In the clearing before the buildings of the reservation headquarters, Lance Costigan knelt over the body of a young brave; in his home on the edge of Bismarck, Jethro Clute planted his heels on his desk and faced Luke Quince who was seated on the other side of the desk.

Jethro Clute was obese and hirsute. He was fifty and a lawyer with a flourishing practice in Bismarck. Behind him was a chequered career on various sections of the frontier — one which would stand very little serious investigation.

Luke Quince was, physically, the lawyer's opposite. He was tall, lean, clean-shaven and thirty-six. Quince had a gash of a mouth under a blade of a nose and his eyes were icy-blue, cold, killer's eyes. He was clad entirely in black and the bulky prominence under his frock-coat, in the region of his waist belt, was caused by a holstered frontier model Colt. Like Clute, Quince also had a chequered career in his wake, equally one which would allow of but little inquiry.

The wilder frontier days had known Luke Quince as a trigger-happy, slug-slamming kid. The gun-towns of Abilene, Dodge and Tombstone had known him and heard his guns in those red-stained days. Quince had been one of a few of the old hot-lead breed to survive the range-wars, the rival cow-camp gun-fests and the lead-slashed bar room brawls of those wide-open days and seen the gradual settlement of the frontier. Like so many of those who were left of the old gun-heavy crews, he had moved with the dwindling frontier. He was a gunslinger and could no more hang up his artillery than a painter can lay down his brush or a poet his pen. So, Quince still drifted into any place there was trouble as a natural consequence and here he was — a henchman of crafty Jethro Clute, acting the part of a respectable lawyer's clerk by day, partner in a gun-running concern by night.

Clute settled his heels on his desk and snicked the end off a large cigar. His nose was bulbous, his eyes small and his whisker-fringed mouth buck-toothed.

'So you don't care for Shaintuck, Luke,' he grated.

'I don't,' replied the other. 'Shaintuck's an old-timer, he's too fond of booze an' the old ham-fisted methods. This ain't Arizona in the '70s, things are different these days, they have Indian police on the reservations for one thing an' they ain't all dumb clucks! The fact that the authorities found those rifles at Standin' Rock proved that Shaintuck an' his pals ain't takin' any powerful good precautions in cachin' their weapons. I figure you could have found slicker operators than those *hombres* to get the guns into the redskin territory.'

'That Standing Rock cache was the only one they found,' answered Clute, puffing on the cigar. 'I guess that ain't so bad in the length of time we've been pushing the weapons into the reservations!'

'Bad enough,' growled Quince. 'Listen, Jethro, I been keepin' my ears open about that find at Standin' Rock an' I heard plenty whispered here an' there. It seems the Indian police an' soldiers got wind of the cached rifles from a drunken Indian. In another couple of days, those Winchesters would have been in the hands of Sittin' Bull's bucks, but a drunken Indian gave the game away. Think of that — an Indian who'd been drinkin' firewater — you know Shaintuck's old reputation, an' a redskin in the vicinity where Eben Shaintuck's operatin' gets drunk an' gives the authorities the word about the rifles. I told you before, Jethro, wherever Shaintuck goes Indians get pickled!'

Jethro Clute hit the desk top a savage kick with a boot-heel.

'I distinctly told that old crow he was not to peddle any of his rot-gut booze to the redskins! Any money an' pay-dirt pokes those Indians have lyin' around we want in exchange for rifles. If Shaintuck has set up a still an' is makin' a private income out of whiskey-runnin', I'll show him who's runnin' this business! The ghost-dance mania will take care of the Indians' temperament without Shaintuck helpin' out with his lousy booze!' In his excitement, the carefully cultivated speech Clute employed in his capacity as lawyer began to slip and he lapsed into the coarser usage of the frontier.

Luke Quince gave him a cold-eyed smile.

'I'll bet my boots, Jethro, that Shaintuck an' his sidekicks, Inskip an' Moate, are runnin' a booze-can somewhere up near the agencies. Like I

warned you before, I knew Eben Shaintuck back in the Arizona days. Wherever
that *hombre* went, there was a trail of
drunk-crazy Apaches behind him!'

'Maybe you're right,' grunted Jethro
Clute. 'I think Mr Jethro Clute, the
well-known and respectable Bismarck
lawyer, will take a little vacation up near
the Indian lands — even if midwinter is
not quite the right time for a holiday!'

'You mean you want to find out first
hand if Shaintuck an' his pals are
double-dealin' you by peddlin' whiskey
on their own account?'

'Quite! The arrival of their boss and
his — er — clerk might shake them into
the realization that they have only one
job to do and it's not to sell whiskey to
the redskins to line their own pockets!'

'Yeah!' smirked Luke Quince, his
lean face moulded into a stiff grin. 'I
guess I can help you point that out to
those three *hombres*!' As he spoke, he
twitched a nervous hand towards the
bulky object under his black coat at the
region of his waist belt.

Lance Costigan knelt over the prone body of the young Indian. He gasped when he saw the death-contorted features, for they were those of Big Tree, only son of Chief White Buffalo and elder brother of Eloise Sun-on-Water. The young brave had three ugly bullet-holes, still welling blood, in his naked chest.

Costigan looked up at the silent faces of the Indians crowding around the corpse. In the background, the squatting squaws were chanting the mournful death-dirge into the whining, chill-edged wind.

The tall figure of old White Buffalo, wearing a multicoloured blanket and a tall, feathered head-dress, stood close to the dead man, his slightly-built, lovely daughter standing at his side. Lance rose and faced the old chief. He asked in the Sioux dialect:

'What is the meaning of this, my father — why do I find my brother, Big Tree, lying here in death?'

White Buffalo stood silent for an instant, staring with solemn and eagle-keen eyes into the face of the half-breed.

'White man's work,' he rumbled at length. 'My son was killed by a white man. He was killed near my camp, on the creek beyond the hill yonder. We brought him here so we can show him to Agent Folinsbee and he will tell the Blue-coats of this.'

Eloise moved towards Lance, a willowy creature in a buckskin dress, her dark cloud of hair braided neatly at the nape of her neck.

'It's terrible, Lance,' she said in English. 'Big Tree was found by a hunting party after they heard shots from a clump of trees. They saw a horseman — a white man — ride out of the trees at a gallop and head east. They were on foot, so could not give chase. They found my brother in the trees — dead.'

'How was he dressed, the white man?' asked Lance, urgently.

Eloise pushed a middle-aged Indian forward.

'Little Squirrel was in the party, he can tell you.'

'This white man — was he wearing a yellow coat?' asked the half-breed in the language of the Sioux. The Indian nodded.

'A yellow coat, yes, and riding a mustang taken from Big Tree. We found the white man's horse dead in the trees — shot. Big Tree had a rifle near his body, a new one. It seems he shot the white man's horse and the white man took his.'

Costigan nodded. So it was Shaintuck's partner, the fellow with the Confederate belt-buckle who had tried to dry-gulch him only that morning. Whatever had happened in that clump of trees close to White Buffalo's camp had something to do with the shady activities of Eben Shaintuck and his companions — and a new rifle was involved. To Costigan, it looked as though the fellow in the yellow slicker had been trying to interest Big Tree in new Winchesters. He had been friendly with White Buffalo's son, but knew the young buck to be, like many of his generation, a hot head fired by wild hopes of a return to the old plains-roving life of their fathers, free from the fetters of the reservation.

It was possible, Lance thought, that Big Tree had been bargaining for that new Winchester in the clump of trees and something flared up between Yellow Slicker and the Indian — a something Yellow Slicker had settled with bullets.

His train of thought was broken by a gravel-voiced cackle and a small, wizened and mud-daubed figure shoved itself through the silent group of Indians. He wore the painted streaks of a medicine-man and flourished a shaman's — wizard's — rattle made of a dried hide bag on the end of a stick. With this, he made a gesture over the body of Big Tree.

'This is an omen, son of a white father and Indian woman,' rasped the

43

medicine-man. 'This is an omen to the people of White Buffalo! It is sent by the Great Spirit to show them how evil is the work of the white man. The people of White Buffalo must join the remainder of the Hunkpapa Sioux in the preparation for the coming of the ghost-gods. They must dance the dances and sing the songs and wait until the Great Spirit sends his messengers to tell us the day of the white man is over. The people of White Buffalo must join their brothers in the ghost-dances, or they will have no share in the happy hunting days that are to come when there are no more whites to kill off the buffalo and steal the land of the Indians . . . '

Lance listened to the *shaman's* wild tirade unmoved. He knew the grotesque Indian to be Owl-in-the-Morning, an upstart medicine-man whose power had been greatly curtailed by the wise ruling of Chief White Buffalo. Doubtless, the wizened little medicine-man saw the outbreak of ghost-dancing as crafty old

Sitting Bull, over at Standing Rock, saw it: an opportunity for the medicine-men to regain their old influence over the tribes.

'Silence!' rapped old White Buffalo, in a voice of thunder. 'You talk with the twisted tongue of a liar, Owl-in-the-Morning! This is no place for the foolish talk of a *shaman*. This is work for the Blue-coats of the white man's law!'

'The white man's law,' echoed Owl-in-the-Morning, baring his broken stumps of teeth. 'Soon there will be no white man's law — soon there will be no white men!'

'Be silent!' ordered White Buffalo again, his stern old eyes flashing menacingly. 'I will have no more of your medicine talk — go back to your tepee, Owl-in-the-Morning!'

The *shaman* slunk away into the crowd of Sioux but Lance noticed the uneasy expressions on the faces of many of the usually wooden-faced red-men, as though certain of them had been affected by the old wizard's talk of the death of Big Tree being an omen. He wondered how much longer White Buffalo's restraining influence would keep his people free of the ghost-dance mania and whether old Owl-in-the-Morning knew anything of what went on that morning between Big Tree and Eben Shaintuck's partner in the yellow slicker.

His train of thought was distracted by the arrival of a white man who shoved his way through the crowd and stood at his shoulder. He was a medium-sized man with a scrubby beard and side-whiskers framing a wrinkle-etched face. He was Joe Folinsbee, agent at the Spring River reservation.

'A bad business, Costigan!' said he in brittle tones. 'A damned bad business!'

'Yeah,' grunted Lance, remembering that, like old Sergeant Zeb Dockery, he disliked this man for no reason he could put his finger on.

'I've been tryin' to telegraph the Indian police over at Standin' Rock,'

Folinsbee said. 'I couldn't get any reply — maybe that big wind last night blew the wire down somewhere!'

'That's darned inconvenient at a time like this,' observed Lance, casting his eyes down to the dead Indian. 'Any idea who did it?'

'Not an idea in the world, Costigan — the Indians say it was a white man — '

'You say that as if the Indians usually lie to you, Folinsbee. I happen to believe them!'

'Sure!' said Joe Folinsbee, quickly, casting a sly look at Lance and remembering that he was speaking to a man who was half-Indian. 'Sure, I guess it could've been a white man!'

'I guess it could,' Lance murmured, bending over the body once more. Those wounds looked as though they had been inflicted with a six-gun, fired at close quarters, he thought to himself. He sniffed suddenly, then knelt a little nearer the dead brave's head. Watched by the group of Sioux, he put his nose close to Big Tree's mouth, twisted open in frozen death-agony, and sniffed again.

He rose solemnly and said to the Indian agent: 'You better have a couple of your men tote him into one of the buildin's an' cover him with a blanket. Let's you an' me go to your office, so we can have a little chat!'

Agent Folinsbee darted him a quick, sidelong look.

'Okay,' he agreed.

As they turned to walk towards the log-constructed office, Lance caught sight of Eloise's grief-clouded, but still lovely face watching him with a curious light in the dark, lustrous eyes.

In the agent's littered office, Folinsbee inquired: 'What do you want to talk about, Costigan?'

Lance produced his cowboy's sack of 'makings' from under his slicker and began to roll a cigarette before answering slowly and studiedly:

'Mainly firewater, Folinsbee.'

'Firewater? What do you mean?'

'Don't act dumb, Folinsbee. I mean

whiskey, booze, the stuff that makes Indians into lunatics! Big Tree had some shortly before his death — I could smell it in his mouth! You're agent here, I want to know how firewater comes to be on your reservation!'

Joe Folinsbee's mouth quavered and he shuffled his feet uneasily.

'Now see here, Costigan, I know you're ridin' the reservations on army orders, but that don't give you no right to talk to me as though I was in on a whiskey-runnin' deal.'

'I didn't say you were but, since you put that kind of construction on what I did say — are you?'

Agent Folinsbee jumped visibly.

'No, I ain't. I been at this post for two years an' there's been no complaints against me — ask the Indian department if you think I'm a liar!'

'A vigilant agent don't allow bad whites to bring whiskey to his reservation,' Lance observed. ' 'Specially when this ghost-dance craze has the majority of the Sioux by the ears!'

'There ain't no big fence around this reservation,' the agent snapped. 'I only got two or three helpers an' I can't be every place at once — I can't help some white renegades gettin' into the camps once in a while!'

'Sure,' agreed Costigan in a more subdued tone, but fixing Joe Folinsbee with his unwavering, jet-black eyes. 'I guess you can't at that. What're you goin' to do about reporting the killing — your telegraph bein' out of order an' all?'

'Send a rider to Standin' Rock or Fort Yates, I guess,' shrugged Folinsbee.

'Then don't bother your head about it,' Costigan replied. 'I'm headin' back in that direction. I'll take the news to the army about young Big Tree's death. You keep a wide eye open for guns an' whiskey — an' ghost-dancin'. Keep a look out for trouble from that old *shaman* Owl-in-the-Morning; he's got a bite from the ghost-dance bug an' some of the Sioux are ready to fall for his wild talk.'

Joe Folinsbee gave a grunt that could have meant anything. Lance wondered whether the bewhiskered little agent knew anything about Yellow Slicker and whatever deal went on between the chief's son and he in that clump of trees near White Buffalo's camp on the creek bottom. Maybe he and old Zeb Dockery were wrong in tagging a man for a 'bad white' with nothing to go on save his crafty looks — but then again, a man developed a kind of instinct when he'd seen his share of renegade whites!

Nodding a curt goodbye to Folinsbee, Lance turned on his heel and left the office. Outside, the first flakes of the snow that had been threatening all morning were beginning to fall, peppering the area around the reservation headquarters with a feathery whiteness that drifted on the keen wind.

The squaws still sat around in shapeless, chanting bundles.

Eloise Sun-on-Water, a wild-rose with the swirling white flakes flurrying about her, was standing close to the door of the office. She advanced on Lance and placed a gentle copper-skinned hand on his arm.

'Lance. You know about the whiskey, don't you? I saw you smell Big Tree's mouth!' she said in English.

'I know he had whiskey shortly before being shot,' Lance replied. 'What can you tell me about whiskey finding its way to the reservation?'

'It was brought here regularly by three men. Big Tree was beginning to get fond of it. I tried to dissuade him from drinking when I first found out about it. Somewhere, he met up with these men and they'd bring it to him, meeting him in the clump of trees. Whenever I spoke to my brother about his drinking, he told me to be off on women's business and to leave him alone. I followed him twice to the stand of trees and hid, watching him buy whiskey from the white men. The first time, there were three of them, the second time, two.'

Lance compressed his lips. 'Three

white men,' he murmured. 'I'll describe them, Eloise; one was old with a grizzly chin, the other two were young and looked like drifting cowhands!'

'Yes!' replied the Sioux girl. 'You know something about them?'

'I know something, but not enough! I know that one of the younger men is Big Tree's murderer and the same man tried to kill me this morning on my way here. Probably that was because he was runnin' from here an' saw me headed this way. He tried to pick me off so I wouldn't find out about your brother's death, but failed. Did Big Tree ever take any of his friends on these whiskey-buying meetin's?'

'No. He was growing more surly and solitary every day and he always seemed to keep the rendezvous with the white men alone. I've been terribly worried about the business.'

'Did your father know about Big Tree's drinkin'?'

'No. I daren't tell him; he would have punished Big Tree severely if he ever found out about the whiskey. They already quarrelled on one occasion when father thought my brother was paying too much attention to Owl-in-the-Morning's talk of the coming of the ghost-gods.'

A frown bit deep into Lance's bronzed forehead. 'You mean Big Tree was falling for that crazy talk?' he inquired.

'Yes. He was beginning to be influenced by the ghost-dance mania and Owl-in-the-Morning's talk of the prophecies of Wovoka. You know how hot-headed Big Tree was about some things — carrying on the fight against the whites, in particular!'

'He wasn't alone in that, Eloise. A lot of young braves feel that way and it's only natural, after all. I'm worried about the fact that some of the younger bucks showed signs of being taken in by old Owl's talk back there a few minutes ago. Your father has managed to hold off the dancing outbreaks so far, but maybe he won't be able to do so for much longer with fellows like Owl going around talkin' wild nonsense!'

'That's my worry,' Eloise replied. 'Father regards this dancing craze as one of Sitting Bull's methods of stirring up trouble against the whites. He's lost faith in Sitting Bull, like most of the Hunkpapa Sioux. He'd far sooner see his people living in peace on the reservation than have them shot down by the soldiers.'

The Indian girl's large dark eyes were melancholy pools in her lovely, snow-touched features. Lance rested a strong and reassuring hand on her shoulder.

'Your father's a wise and a good man, Eloise, I'm sure he'll be able to hold off the spread of the dancing to Spring River reservation. It's gripped the other Indian camps firmly and the Sioux are dancin' themselves to exhaustion every day — some have even died. Don't be scared about the soldiers shootin' your people. The President sent them to Dakota because of the fuss some folk started raisin' when the ghost-dance craze first broke. Jim McLaughlin, the agent over at Standin' Rock, told Washington that there was no need for troops an' suggested that the Sioux should be left to carry on with their dancin' until spring. By that time, he figured, the Indians would be tired of it an' quit when they didn't see any signs of their ghost-gods arrivin'. I figure Jim's right, but the soldiers have been sent in an' I guess that's added fuel to the flames so far as the young bucks who want to fight soldiers like their fathers did are concerned. It adds to my troubles, too, because troops bein' on the scene makes the hot-head braves want to grab weapons equal to theirs — so bringin' in the bad whites who like to dabble in gun-runnin'!'

Eloise raised her dark eyes to look squarely into his face. When she spoke, there was an unusual husky edge to her voice.

'Lance, be careful when you're dealing with those bad whites! I — I don't want you to end the same way as my brother!'

'I'll watch my step, Eloise,' he replied; wondering at the lump that suddenly arose in his throat as he looked into her snow-wet face. 'I'll take care, Eloise. I already have a score to settle with the guy in the yellow slicker for tryin' to gun me from cover this mornin'; now, I want to get him for the murder of Big Tree!'

Eloise Sun-on-Water, without any regard for the Indians who still lingered around the buildings of the reservation centre or the wailing, blanketed squaws, suddenly threw her slender arms round the half-breed's neck, pressed herself close to him and, standing on tip-toe, kissed him.

'Take care!' she whispered hoarsely as she released the grip of her encircling arms. Then she turned and ran.

Lance Costigan stood, rooted to the spot, watching her retreating back until the lithe, willowy figure in the simple buckskin dress was swallowed by the increasing swirl of wind-driven snow.

4

Before leaving the reservation, Lance stopped in at the commissary store and shared a lunch of hot coffee and stew with its keeper, an old acquaintance. Over the meal, they chatted about developments on the agencies, Lance entering into the conversation only half-heartedly.

Uppermost in his mind was the killing of Big Tree and his desire to track down the young man with the yellow slicker and the rebel belt-buckle. Yet, despite the weight of the murder of his Indian friend, a part of his mind was jubilant at the kiss just given to him by Eloise.

For months now, he had known that the feeling he held for the wild-rose creature of Silver Spring reservation was the real thing — the love of man for woman which a man of his calibre and calling only allowed to enter his mind when he had time to wonder what life had to offer. Resting up by some cattle-trail water-hole or pillowing his head on his saddle during the lonesome, star-flecked nights of the roundups, Lance had wondered whether gentle Eloise was the woman for him.

Like the shy-of-women cowpuncher he was at heart, he had stood around, thrilling to the simple charm of the Indian girl and never made an effort to tell her how he felt. And now, by all the powers, she'd made the first move — and kissed him.

There was a warmth, caused by something other than the stew and coffee, in him as he swung into the saddle of his gelding and rode out of the reservation. He fought off romantic, daydreaming notions as he headed back in the direction of Black Boulder. That had been the direction in which the man in the yellow slicker had been heading when he hazed out of the rock outcrop that morning on the Indian pony. He had not a notion in the world where to start looking for Eben Shaintuck and his two gun-heavy companions, but he vowed he would seek them out if it meant riding clear over the Canadian line and searching as far as the North Pole. And, when he found them, he would hand out more than the fist-punishment he had given them in the Dakota Palace the previous night!

Meanwhile, there was no harm in looking in at Black Boulder on the way to Fort Yates, where he would report the killing of Big Tree to the Army and Indian police.

Costigan rode through the swirling curtain of snow, a heavily muffled figure in his quilted slicker, keeping his head, in its broad-brimmed hat, held well down. The energetic gelding was making good speed, in spite of the snow, which was now falling in a thicker, whirling curtain of white. A little apprehensively, Lance thought that this fall showed all the signs of blowing up into a furious Dakota blizzard. He spurred the horse onward, anxious to reach Black Boulder before the threatened storm was unleashed.

He had been riding for about half-an-hour when the sound of hoofs, snow-muffled, but pounding nearer quite distinctly, assailed his ears. He stiffened in the saddle and waited, listening. Out of the white smother of swirling snow behind him, the sound of the approaching horse grew louder. The hoofs sounded unshod, like the hoofs of an Indian mustang. Whoever was riding towards Costigan through the snow-storm was making good speed.

He saw the figure of the mounted man come suddenly out of the milky-blurred swirl; a slicker-bundled, white-rimed anonymous figure on a snow-plastered mustang.

A cold stab of fear rose suddenly in Lance when he saw that the man was flourishing a rifle — and, even now, in the act of levelling the weapon at him.

Costigan touched his spurs to the

gelding, forcing it to lope into the midst of the wind-flurried curtain of snow before the man on the mustang fired. He crouched low in the saddle, almost lying on the horse's neck.

The bark of the rifle came bellowing out of the milk-white world around Lance and he heard the slug go whanging somewhere over his head.

'*Twice in one day!*' he snorted. '*Two attempts to put my light out with a Winchester!*'

He whirled the gelding with savage speed, fumbling under his slicker and grabbing his six-gun as he did so.

Out of the whiteness came the sound of a round being pumped into the breech of a repeater, then the unknown mustang-rider emerged from the swirling snow.

Costigan fired first and the other went screaming out of his saddle. The scared mustang went trotting away to become lost in the driving sheets of snow.

Lance saw the man on his knees in

the snow and heard him spluttering harshly in pain. His broad-brimmed Stetson was still on his head and he was still cloaked with anonymity because of the white drift of snow flakes which rendered his features indistinguishable. Down there, kneeling in the thickening snow, he levelled the Winchester at Costigan once more. Lance canted his body in the saddle quickly and triggered his Colt at the other's head mercilessly.

The kneeling figure, still clutching the rifle, crumpled down into the snow without a sound. Briefly, he kicked his life out while the snow about him became coloured with a spreading pool of crimson.

Costigan dismounted, slung his reins over the gelding's head to prevent the animal from wandering and trudged through the ankle-deep snow to the still form of the man he had shot.

He knelt over the slicker-bundled corpse, turned it over so that he could see the face of the man who had tried to kill him. The flat-crowned Stetson fell from the dead man's head as he did so, making identification easier.

The snow-crusted, slack-jawed face of the dead man was that of Agent Joe Folinsbee, of Spring River Agency!

'*Folinsbee!*' breathed Lance. So, both he and Zeb Dockery had been right in mistrusting this man!

He squatted in the snow for a long time, holding the dead Indian Agent and watching the flakes of snow form a crust on the lifeless features.

He tried to reason out why Joe Folinsbee should come after him with a rifle in the hope of gunning him down on the prairie.

Then the reason hit him hard.

The whiskey- and gun-running, the killing of Big Tree — Folinsbee had been in on them and he did not want news of what had so recently happened at Spring River reservation to reach the military. His story of the telegraph being out of action was probably so much hogwash. Lance's offer to take news of the killing of Chief White Buffalo's son to the authorities had come as an unwelcome surprise to the agent. But he had obviously figured he would remedy that by fixing things so that the half-breed did not reach Standing Rock — by overtaking him in the thick of the snowstorm on a swift Indian pony and killing him.

Costigan reflected that, if Folinsbee's scheme had succeeded, his body would doubtless be ditched into some creek bottom.

So, Folinsbee, Shaintuck and the latter's two partners were in cahoots! Now what?

The half-breed looked quickly about him. The wind-driven fury of the snow was increasing. As he had feared it was turning into one of the icy, wind-slashed blizzards of the north-western plains. Every second spent dallying here increased his chances of becoming lost, as even the most experienced wanderer of the prairie trails could become lost in such a blizzard. Yet, he could not leave the body of Folinsbee here for prowling coyotes who would come out after the storm.

He had killed the Indian agent in self-defence, but he knew the demands of the law. A coroner would have to hold an inquest on the corpse and Lance would be required to give evidence of the shooting. He himself desired to do this in order that his side of the story would be made known.

He decided that he would have to carry the body through the storm to Black Boulder, the nearest settlement with a US Marshal in residence as well as a justice of the peace. Working quickly, but staggering under the frequent buffets of the driving wind, he hefted the body of Joe Folinsbee up across his gelding's neck. Then, he mounted and spurred the double-loaded horse forward into the white smother. The gelding made slow progress through the fetlock-deep snow and Lance rode in a forward-crouching huddle, fighting for his breath against the icy swirls of wind-carried flakes.

His quilted slicker, his hat and his features were soon deeply snow-rimmed and the still form of Folinsbee was a white-plastered bundle across the flake-whitened neck of the horse. Costigan spurred the bay gelding frequently.

The wind was a screeching demon scything the wide plains with an ice-edged blade, threatening to buffet the rider, his grisly burden and the horse itself over into the deepening snow at every other minute. Onward plodded the plucky gelding, trudging through the drifting snow which was now nearer its knees than its fetlocks. It snorted steamy ribbons of breath into the milky swirl and chomped on its ice-cold steel bit.

Fearful of the overburdened animal becoming exhausted, Lance dismounted and led the gelding by the rein, trudging knee-deep in the cloying, thickening white blanket that covered the plains.

In the wind-borne swirl of white, he lost all conception of time and place and became a mechanical thing struggling onward, as is the way with those who defy blizzards or deserts. For an uncountable length of time, his only concern was to put one leg before the other. Benumbed, he trudged on, not even remembering where he was going, mindful only of the fact that he must lead the horse, that he must keep moving forward, that he must not stop or fall — to freeze to death in the fury of the storm.

'Onward — slowly — mechanically. Clutch the reins — don't stop — it's death to stop!'

Through the whirling curtains of snow, he floundered in a half-delirious fashion; a hundred phantom voices borne on the wind seemed to whisper into his ears.

It was a slight abatement of the blizzard that brought him to his senses. His body was aching from top to toe. He was a white-plastered thing like a walking snowman. But he was still clutching the reins of the horse. The animal, like himself, was covered with caked snow and was almost all-in. The stiff, white object draped over its neck had little about it to show it had once been a living, breathing man.

Costigan staggered on through the lessening wind, leading the gallant gelding onward, shoving one painful leg before the other as though each weighed a ton.

He had no idea where he was and was completely without a notion as to how long the fury of the blizzard had lasted. He had become an automaton during its peak and might have plunged on for hours, covering the same area of ground in a circle. One thing was certain and that was that he could no longer be on the trail to Black Boulder.

What appeared to be a whitened mound loomed out of the diminishing curtains of snow. It resolved itself into a crumbling sod-shack, against which the snow had blown in deep drifts.

It was painful to Lance to even attempt to think, but he recollected that he had once passed such a deserted homestead months before — and it was miles from the Black Boulder trail.

He staggered towards the crumbling shack, gratefully. It was partly caved-in, but had a substantial portion of roof left. The place held an air of dejection, silently telling of the hopeful 'sodbuster' who had settled on his claim of land the previous spring — one of the many Scandinavian settlers who flooded into the North-West, perhaps, or a factory worker from the east who had scrabbled together the price of a claim. The dream of a farm had been half-solidified here — for a time. Someone had built the sod-shanty — a temporary home — someone had broken the tough plain with a plough; raised a little corn and maize, milked his cow and fed his pigs. The dream had never solidified completely. The homestead had never become more than a nebulous half-formed and pathetic thing.

The winds of autumn came.

The plough-broken land fell prey to the clutching grasp of the prairie winds, which carried with it the homesteader's dream. The coming of winter had brought the frost and snow and the sodbuster, struggling to recapture something of a dream that had already gone, had become disillusioned and went away to follow a life he understood.

Lance Costigan stumbled into what was left of the shanty, pulling the horse and its burden with him.

The four walls were still intact and there was enough roof left at one end to provide shelter from the snow and wind. The gelding flopped into a kneeling position almost as soon as it entered the sheltering walls, its nostrils working in a steaming, grateful snort.

Lance, moving stiffly and wearily, dragged the body of Folinsbee from the gelding and laid the stiffened form in a corner. He pulled his bedroll and warsack from behind the saddle where they had been protected from the snow by a tarp sheet, then unbuckled the saddle and removed it from the animal. The horse rolled over and lay on its side, thankfully free of the burden.

The half-breed produced his cow-hand's cooking gear and his few canned provisions; oats for the horse and coffee from his war-sack. He found some broken spars of dry timber lying around, built a fire, took his camp-dixie out into the abating storm and filled it with snow to melt down over the flames. Within a quarter-of-an-hour he had watered the gelding, fed it oats, prepared a steaming tin-cup of coffee and heated a can of stew.

Within a further twenty minutes, he was stretched in his bedroll by the embers of his dying fire, sleeping deeply and dreamlessly.

5

Lance Costigan awoke sluggishly from his deep sleep. The rosy flush of a new dawn was high in the wintry sky and the snow had stopped. He had no knowledge of how long he had slept, but it had been early evening when he discovered the crumbling sod-shanty. He shook his head and rubbed the sleep from his eyes. When he could think with clarity, he realised that he had slept for part of an evening and a whole night. Judging by the feeble, wintry morning light which now invaded the ruined shanty through its caved-in roof, it was somewhere about five o'clock.

The bay gelding was standing in the corner, cropping at some sparse grass which struggled among the tumbled sods. The stiff form of Joe Folinsbee was stretched grotesquely in the shadows.

Lance struggled out of his bedroll. He was stiff, but refreshed by sleep. The fire was completely dead, but he scrabbled about among the scattered debris of the shack, found more dry wood and set about preparing a new fire. He made a cupful of coffee, sipped it slowly and felt its warmth seeping into his body. Then he stood at the low, crumbling door of the shanty and tried to find his bearings.

The white carpet of snow had changed the face of the plains, but a distant drift of hills and stand of black-jacks gave him some notion of his position. With a shock, he realised how far he had drifted from the trail to Black Boulder during the nightmare of the blizzard. He knew that his way lay in the direction of the straggle of hills and he could cut off several miles of riding by heading over the knoll on which the black-jacks stood against the wintry, frost-polished dawn.

Having watered the bay gelding with melted snow, saddled up and slung the corpse of the Indian agent from Spring River over its neck, he rode out of the deserted homestead claim. He rode the snow-blanketed plains slowly, sparing his mount.

An hour later he was riding up the slopes of the black-jack studded knoll. Morning had blossomed fully now, and the December sunshine splashed a weak, honey-coloured sheen over the whiteness of the snow-spread landscape.

In the midst of the trees atop the knoll, Lance rested his horse. Down on the other side of the knoll, its sides thick with winter-denuded black-jacks, aspen and live-oaks, swept a deep valley. Lance knew the place well, Lost Valley was the name that had been given to it.

It was a place of evil repute. Some superstition, lost in Indian lore, had clung about it since the days when the Sioux roamed the plains unmolested by the whites. No one had ever settled here save one man. He was a half-crazed gold seeker who came with the rush to Dakota when the rumour of gold in the

Black Hills captured men's imagination. Apparently, he had found no fabulous strike down there in the Black Hills and had drifted up north, finding Lost Valley.

Something, perhaps a chance-found nugget, caused him to stay in that Indian-forbidden place. He built a cabin on the timber-dotted side of the valley and scrabbled for the elusive yellow metal in vain for months. Wandering plainsmen came to the valley in the first days of the spring following the old prospector's arrival there. They found what was left of him lying on his bunk in his cabin. The hard hand of the North-Western winds had locked the valley, finding the half-crazy old man without provisions for the long months of snow.

Thereafter, the evil reputation of the place was intensified.

The cabin fell into ruin and both Indian and white avoided the valley.

Lance Costigan looked down into the snow-spread valley, seeking the spot among the stark trees where he knew the remains of the cabin to be. He sniffed suddenly as an acrid tang came to his nostrils.

He narrowed his coal-black eyes against the glare of the sun reflected from the snow and caught sight of two thin plumes of smoke curling up from the cabin site, one a lighter grey than the other. From this distance he could make out the cabin quite clearly, squatting on the far side of the valley. But it was no longer a ruined cabin. Someone had re-roofed it recently and the newness of the peeled logs on top of the small building was apparent in the glare of the wintry sunshine.

The wind was blowing the smoke which issued from the cabin toward the tree-tipped knoll on which the rider with his grisly burden rested. The acrid tang was from the lighter plume of smoke and Lance was able to give a name to it.

'*Corn*!' he grunted. 'Someone's operatin' a still down there — makin' corn-whiskey!'

The second, thicker drift of smoke came from the ordinary tin stovepipe which canted crazily out of the cabin roof, but Lance could discern that the lighter smoke issued from a smoke-stack on a smaller, newly-built portion of the shack.

'So that's where Shaintuck an' his pals make their rot-gut!' the half-breed mused. 'An' I guess that's where they keep their stock of rifles for trade with the Indians!'

He backed the gelding deeper into the stand of black-jacks so he would not be seen from the cabin. Grimly, he thought that, even now, the youngster with the Confederate belt who had killed Big Tree and attempted to ambush him the day before would be down in that cabin. Sitting like a statue, with the body of the dead man slumped over the neck of his mount, he watched the valley and the cabin from the tree-grown eminence.

He saw a distance-diminished figure emerge from the wooden building and sling the contents of a bucket into the trees. It was a bent, bowlegged figure and Lance knew it to be that of Eben Shaintuck. He knew a moment of strong temptation. He wanted to ride down into the silence of Lost Valley with a blazing gun — blazing with vengeance for the murder of Big Tree and the attempt on his own life back there in the outcrop of the badlands.

But that would have to wait. He had other business in Black Boulder first; then he would ride back to the cabin in Lost Valley.

He wheeled the gelding about and started down the offside of the knoll so that he could not be seen from the valley.

Still riding slowly, he began the long sweep around the valley that would bring him into Black Boulder.

★   ★   ★

Owing to the snow-blocked trails, the afternoon stage was late in arriving at Black Boulder.

79

It came jouncing through the snow puddles that spread across the wide dirt street of the town with a jingle of trappings and its team snorting. Wrenching on the leads, the driver loosed a hoarse yell and shoved his boot hard against the wooden lever which applied the brake, bringing the coach to a slithering, squelching stop in the mud outside the stage-line office.

The driver, a gnarled oldster, began to sling mail and baggage from the top of the coach down to the stage agent who was standing on the plank-walk outside his office. The door of the stagecoach swung open and the passengers began to alight.

There were only two this trip and both gentlemen, it seemed. The loafers of Black Boulder, to whom the arrival of the coach was always a novelty, stood around watching the pair of black-garbed men who climbed down from the vehicle.

One was fat and had a luxuriant spread of whiskers. The other was younger and clean-shaven. He had an intensive glitter to his eyes which might have belonged to a fanatical preacher — or a killer.

Jethro Clute, the fat one, sniffed and regarded the single street of Black Boulder. He viewed the motley cluster of false-fronted wooden buildings, awnings and garishly painted signs with a disdain which conveyed to the loafers of Black Boulder that he was unused to such primitive surroundings. His attitude caused Luke Quince to smile a purely mental and sardonic smile to himself. To judge from the airs and graces the Bismarck lawyer put on, no one would ever imagine that, fifteen years before, he had been the guest of the Governor of Arizona in the territorial jail at Yuma. He had been there under his own name, which was not Clute. That, in fact, was where Luke Quince had first met him.

One man on the street of Black Boulder showed an unusual interest in the two who had just alighted from the stage. He was a grey-haired sergeant of

81

cavalry who sat his horse off to one side of the stage office.

Sergeant Zeb Dockery was prompted by the sight of the black-clad pair to send his thoughts rifling through the memories stored up over years of service in the United States Army. The faces of the pair set him to thinking of the early days of the campaign against Cochise and his Apaches. There had been bad whites galore down in Arizona in those days. One of them, a flabby-faced gun-runner who had been caught and sentenced for his friendliness towards the Apaches — a friendliness which did not stop short of supplying them with weapons with which to fight the soldiers of Uncle Sam. Even a profuse growth of beard did not disguise the flabby face from the keen eye of Zeb Dockery.

Then there was Quince. Quince, the kid gunfighter, who shoved his nose — and his gun — into every ruckus of the border ranges. He had been jailed for manslaughter in one such cow-punchers' flare-up. He was older now, but the added years and parsonical black outfit did little to hide his gunslinger's manner. Nor did the significant bulge around his waist belt escape Dockery.

The old non-com jetted a stream of tobacco-juice into the mud of the street.

'Well, ain't this most interestin',' he thought to himself. 'Here we are on the edge of Injun-trouble an' these two show up just when there's a mess of gun-runnin' in the air. Lance Costigan is sure goin' to find this kind of development plumb fascinatin'! Jerry Cray, the gun-runnin' lawyer from the old Arizony days, an' Luke Quince, who somehow growed to be dry behind the ears without someone lead poisonin' him! Well, well!'

The old soldier's train of thought was suddenly broken off at the sight of a rider entering the puddle-scattered street, allowing his heavily burdened mount to pick its way slowly through the stretches of water and half-melted snow. A copper-skinned man in a wide hat and quilted slicker who rode with the stiff corpse of another man hanging before his saddle.

'I suppose that place over yonder will be as good as any other in this grubby camp,' Jethro Clute, alias Jerry Cray, was saying, nodding his silk-hatted head in the direction of the sign which announced that the Dakota Palace was a combination of saloon and hotel.

Clute was about to cross the street in the direction of the Dakota Palace when Luke Quince grabbed his arm.

'Some kind of commotion goin' on up the street there,' he pointed out. 'That fellow's got a corpse over his cayuse!'

The men from Bismarck watched the excited cluster of Black Boulder folk gathering around the riding figure of the obvious half-Indian who came slowly along the street with his unusual burden.

The copper-skinned man rode without looking to the left or right and without answering the babel of questions fired at him.

'Maybe some bounty-hunter or a badge-carrier bringing in a wanted man,' observed Clute, in his precise lawyer's tones. Then he overheard a man yell:

'Hey, that's Joe Folinsbee from Spring River! Looks like Joe's dead as mutton!'

Jethro Clute cast his tall companion a quick glance.

'Hear that?' he husked. 'Folinsbee was the name of one of the men Shaintuck is dealing with isn't it?'

'Yeah. Injun agent at a reservation called Spring River. Looks like somethin' else has gone wrong with our deal!'

'An' that damned oaf Shaintuck has blundered again, I'll wager,' snorted Clute, forgetting his correct manner in his excitement.

'You hired him, not me,' retorted Luke Quince, curtly. 'You figured he was well-experienced in exchangin' guns for Injun money!'

'Where's he takin' that dead man?'

asked Clute, watching the copper-skinned man dismount over near the far boardwalk.

'Into the marshal's office. See the sign over on the awning there?'

'Let's get over there an' see what it's all about,' urged Clute and the two men from Bismarck began to pick their way through the mud puddles of the street towards the group of Black Boulder citizenry which had gathered around the slicker-bundled man who was now in the act of swinging the half-frozen corpse down from the gelding.

Sergeant Zeb Dockery held his position, sitting his horse with patience that came of years in the saddle. He was out of earshot and could not catch any of the words spoken by the men he remembered from the old days of the Arizona Apache troubles, but he noted that both were showing a lively interest in the arrival of Lance Costigan with his grisly bundle.

No less than anyone else on the street, he was intrigued as to why the half-breed son of his old Indian-scout friend, Malachy Costigan should arrive in town with the dead body of Joe Folinsbee draped over his mount. When he saw the two city-garbed men walk towards the office of Marshal Gantz, he angled his horse across the street and joined the crowd around the law-office, making sure he was close behind the two who had so recently arrived in town.

Marshal Otto Gantz, a big Teutonic figure, was standing on the gallery outside his office. He registered only mild surprise at the arrival of Costigan and his bundle of death. He had been a frontier law-officer for more than twenty years and was inured to sudden death, even in these days which smug folk reckoned were more or less settled.

'How'd he die?' called Gantz, as though men brought corpses to his office every hour of the day.

'Shot,' replied Lance. 'By me — an' I claim self-defence! I brought him in for inquest an' I'd appreciate it if it could

87

be held right now; I'm a busy man with plenty to do!'

'Sure,' agreed Gantz in his matter-of-fact way. He spoke to a small boy in the crowd: 'Tommy, run across to the Horseshoe Saloon an' get Doc Murchison, then run up the street an' bring Judge Wiggs — tell 'em it's urgent!'

Marshal Gantz cast his eyes around the crowd of inquisitive townsfolk. 'I'll want a jury of sober an' sensible men,' he announced. 'You, Fred, you Charlie; an' you, Nels; you, too, Ike an' Sergeant Dockery there . . . ' The marshal went on picking out jurors while Lance toted the body of the Indian agent across the gallery and into the office, where he laid it on a scarred wooden table.

The lawman cleared the crowd away from the front of his office while the jury filed in and stood around, leaning against the walls. Presently old Doc Murchison, in a reasonable sober condition, arrived, with Judge Wiggs.

While the old medico was making his cursory examination of the body,

Sergeant Zeb Dockery moved away from the rest of the jurors and stood close to Lance. He nodded towards the closed door of the law-office.

'There's a couple of gents outside in the crowd you'd be plumb taken with, Lance,' he whispered. 'Just come in on the stage. Two *hombres* I remember from the old Arizona days — both bad whites. Plumb funny they should show up around here when this gun-runnin' trouble is in the wind. See me outside, so we can talk some in private!'

Lance nodded to the old cavalryman.

'Okay,' he agreed in low tones. 'I found where Shaintuck an' his pals are holin' up, by the way. I aim to go there later an' do some hell-raisin'!'

In the background, old Doc Murchison cleared his throat and announced his finding: 'Death due to gunshot wounds — probably instantaneous,' he wheezed.

Judge Wiggs, seated at the marshal's desk, solemnly recorded the medical man's findings on a length of legal paper.

'What can you tell us about this man's death, Mr Costigan?' asked the coroner.

Lance gave his evidence slowly while Judge Wiggs wrote down every word with a scratchy pen.

'I shot him when he came after me during the snowstorm with a rifle. I was ridin' from the Indian reservation at Spring River when he came behind me, firin' on me. I shot him from his saddle in defence of my own life. He tried to fire on me again and I shot him dead.'

'You an' him have any trouble, any quarrel or anythin' like that?' asked Judge Wiggs. 'D'you have any idea why Folinsbee should try to take your life?'

'Yes, sir. I believe he did it to prevent me taking certain news, concerning a recent happening on his reservation, to the authorities.'

'Was this in connection with your work in ridin' the reservations for the

Army and Indian police?' queried the coroner.

'Yes. And that's all I wish to say at this point until I report to the Army at Fort Yates. I claim I shot Joe Folinsbee in self-defence.'

The wizened old judge nodded and turned to the gathered jurymen: 'What's your verdict?' he inquired.

The little collection of Black Boulder citizenry put their heads together and buzzed for a brief instant, then came out of the huddle.

'Shot to death by Lance Costigan while the latter was defendin' his life against armed attack,' announced Nels Olvigg, the storekeeper who had been appointed foreman of the jury.

Old Judge Wiggs gravely wrote the finding on the length of legal paper.

'That's good enough, gentlemen. Marshal Gantz, make arrangements for Folinsbee to be planted in Boot Hill. I guess you'll report his — er — demise to the Indian authorities, Mr Costigan.'

Lance nodded.

Judge Wiggs invited Doc Murchison to join him in a drink over at the Horseshoe Saloon and those concerned took this as notification that the inquest was over.

While the requirements of the law had been in the process of being fulfilled in this informal manner, the door of the marshal's office was closed. Nevertheless, the inquisitive folk on the gallery had heard most of the proceedings through the partly-open window. Among those who secured a place in the crowd within earshot of what was going on in the law-office, were the two black-garbed men from the Bismarck stage. These apparent gentlemen stationed themselves close to the window and exchanged a variety of glances at the words they heard issuing therefrom.

When the door of the office opened and the men concerned in the inquest on the dead agent began to file out, they betook themselves off the gallery fronting the office, headed for the stage office, where their luggage was and thence to the Dakota Palace.

Jethro Clute was in a towering rage, but he managed to hold his ire pent within him until he and his cold-eyed companion booked rooms at the saloon-cum-hotel.

'That half-breed, he's dangerous! He's workin' for the Army — he's killed Folinsbee an' there's no knowin' what's happenin' to our plans!'

Clute's precise lawyer tones, so well known in Bismarck, were slipping badly in his excitement. 'I thought Shaintuck had everythin' foolproof!'

'That damned Shaintuck,' grumbled Luke Quince. 'I told you at the start that he was no kind of guy to handle our affairs out here!'

Clute began to fumble in the carpetbag containing his belongings and eventually produced a sketch-map which he unfolded on a table.

'I intend ridin' out to this Lost Valley place where Shaintuck's supposed to be operatin' from. I want to know whether he's doin' any private business with booze, I want to know why things were bungled at the Pine Ridge Agency, so the rifles were found an' I want like all hell to know what's been happenin' at Spring River for this half-breed to go stickin' his nose into there and wind up shootin' Folinsbee!'

Quince was poring over the map.

'You can't go ridin' out today,' he observed. 'Evenin's comin' on an' Lost Valley is some miles from here across unfamiliar country. Besides, we'll have to hire horses from somewhere.'

'Maybe not today,' retorted Clute. 'But we'll go there first thing in the morning. I want to get to the bottom of the bunglin' that's been goin' on around here!'

'Me, too,' grunted Luke Quince. 'One thing I'd sure admire to do is fix that half-breed *hombre* for keeps.' His thin-lipped mouth under his blade of a nose became stitched back in a cold grin. 'Fact is, Jethro, I got a trigger-itch like I ain't known for a long time comin' on. I have a hunch someone's goin' to have to put a stop to this half-breed's monkey-shines — an' I kind of figure it'll be me!'

Meanwhile, some little way along the street, Lance and old Zeb Dockery were deep in conversation. They were standing on the rough wooden plank-walk outside the Horseshoe Saloon.

'Two gun-runnin' fellers from the Arizona Apache wars you say?' asked the half-breed. 'You sure they're the same men?'

'I'm plumb sure, Lance,' the old cavalryman answered. 'One of them growed a beard since, but he's Cray all right — a renegade lawyer that made himself quite a pile runnin' rifles to Cochise an' his braves before the authorities catched him. The other's a gunslinger named Luke Quince. Had a big reputation on the border when he was just a kid. He used to shove his gun in any place there was room enough to pull the trigger.'

'Quince,' repeated Costigan. 'I've heard of him — he was supposed to be fast.'

'He's fast, all right. Watch out, Lance; I don't figure the arrival of those two birds is unconnected with the Indian trouble up here — could be that they're at the top of the rifle- and booze-runnin' racket.'

'Could be,' mused Lance. 'General Miles figures there's somebody pretty smart at the top an' the smugglin' is not just carried out by local renegades.'

'What were you sayin' about ridin' out to Lost Valley an' makin' trouble for Shaintuck an' his partners?' queried the old sergeant.

'I aim to ride out there tomorrow mornin' an' fix that bunch. They're holed up in that old prospector's cabin there an' they have a still rigged up, you can smell it a mile off. That's where they cook up the lousy rot-gut booze they peddle to the Indians. I want to wreck that still, but that's the least of the chores I have to attend to. One of them galoots, the guy with the rebel belt-buckle I socked in the Palace a couple of nights back, tried to kill me an' he's the guy who killed Big Tree. I want to find out what was goin' on between him an' Big Tree, then I'll even up with him.'

'That's a kind of tall order,' rumbled Zeb. 'You goin' out there on your lonesome an' tacklin' those *hombres*. I told you before that old Shaintuck is pizen. Don't underestimate him or you might wind up as a corpse in Lost Valley! Anyway, what you goin' to do about notifyin' the Army about the deaths of Big Tree an' Folinsbee? Seems to me the situation out at Spring River could be kinda bad without an agent there to keep an eye on the place.'

'It'd be just as bad if Folinsbee was still there — he was runnin' with the gun-peddlers or why else would he try to kill me! Still, he'll have to be replaced. I'll write a letter for you to take to Major Aitchison when you go back to the fort tonight. I'll tell him the whole position.'

'I still figure it's foolish of you to think of stickin' your neck into Lost

Valley on your own,' remarked Zeb Dockery.

But the old non-com knew the black-eyed, copper-skinned rider was every inch like his old man, fiery Malachy Costigan of the days of the real Indian wars — once his mind was made up, it stayed that way!

6

That night, Sergeant Zeb Dockery rode back to Fort Yates with a square of paper in his tunic-pocket. On it was written:

Major W. B. Aitchison, US Army,
Fort Yates, North Dakota.

Sir,
I have to report that Joseph Folinsbee, agent at Spring River Indian reservation, was shot and killed by me on December 12th some distance from the reservation. He attacked me and I shot in self-defence. The process of the law has been carried out and a coroner's verdict returned on the body.

This shooting was the result of Folinsbee overtaking me on the trail and trying to kill me with a rifle. I believe he did this to prevent me informing you of the fact that Big Tree, son of Chief White Buffalo, was murdered at the reservation that same day and that there has been some smuggling of guns and whiskey into the reservation. His story was that he could not contact Fort Yates or Standing Rock because the telegraph wire had been blown down. You will know whether this story is true or not.

I know the killer of Big Tree, but not his name. He is a man in his middle-twenties, clean-shaven, wearing a Confederate Army buckle on his belt. This man, another of about his own age and Eben Shaintuck have a cabin at Lost Valley where they are running a whiskey still and, no doubt, have supplies of weapons there.

Two men, identified to me by Sergeant Dockery as Gerry Cray and Luke Quince, both of whom were involved in gun-running in the

Arizona Apache wars, have lately arrived in Black Boulder. Sergeant Dockery can describe them.

I am going into Lost Valley alone early tomorrow. It is my intention to destroy the whiskey still, look for the supplies of arms and arrest the murderer of White Buffalo's son. The odds are three to one against me. If I should disappear, look for my remains in the Lost Valley vicinity.

Your obedient servant,
Lance Costigan.

Lance wrote the letter while he and Dockery drank together in a quiet corner of the Horseshoe Saloon. Old Zeb was loud in his opinion that Lance was a fool to attempt any action at Lost Valley, but the half-breed would hear none of his objections.

Later, Lance took a room at the Dakota Palace, unaware that the two men Dockery had warned him against were already asleep in two other rooms under that same roof!

* * *

That night also, there was trouble at Spring River.

In White Buffalo's camp down on the creek-bottoms, the blaze of firelight washed a flickering sheen over the Sioux tepees and the bare, snow-festooned trees. Its red and yellow glow painted the grave, image-like faces of the Indians who squatted about, still chanting for Big Tree.

Eloise Sun-on-Water, seated with a group of maidens, got the first hint of trouble when she saw half-a-dozen bucks slip away in the direction of the clump of trees which had been the place of her brother's death. She could not recognise the faces of all the young men who went so furtively into the grove which had been Big Tree's place of rendezvous with the renegade whites, but those she did see caused a cold wash of apprehension to leap within her. There was Blue Pony, Small Dog and Hunting Wolf, young malcontents all.

Her watch on the cluster of trees was broken when a figure in a tattered buffalo-robe came slinking from among the tepees and leapt into the circle of firelight with dramatic suddenness.

It was Owl-in-the-Morning, the old medicine-man, shaking the pebbles of his *shaman's* rattle and blowing a shrill note on an eagle-bone whistle. The chanting ceased abruptly and fire-lit eyes were turned on the prancing figure of the old wizard.

'Aaaeee!' shrilled the old Indian. 'Hear me, children of the plains! Is not the death of Big Tree a warning from the Great Spirit? Is it not time we joined our brothers in the preparation for the coming of the ghost-leaders he is to send to lead the Sioux in their final battle against the white men who have plundered and killed? Has not the white man made promises which he has never kept? Has not the white man said: 'I will place you under the protection of the Great White Father in Washington if you lay down your arms' — and have we not starved under that protection? Begin the ghost-dancing now! Join our brothers of the Hunkpapa Sioux and dance until the ghost-gods come!'

'Silence! Owl-in-the-Morning, twice you have sought to stir my children to rash action!' The words were spoken loudly and sternly by old White Buffalo, rising from his chief's place by the fire. He was a tall, blanketed and leather-crested figure, standing as stern as a totem with his keen eyes flashing in the light of the flames. 'Owl-in-the-Morning, your talk is as meaningless as the talk of a stream running over stones. Yours is the twisted tongue of a liar that would lead my people against the blue-coats and into certain death — '

Owl-in-the-Morning interrupted the chief with another wild screech, he pointed a scrawny hand at White Buffalo. 'White Buffalo is a doubter! The Great Spirit will protect us in our fight against the whites. The secret of making gunpowder will be taken from their heads, their guns will be unable to kill us for our shirts will be rendered proof against their bullets!'

Around the fire, one or two of the more excitable of the tribe were beginning to stir uneasily. Belief and half-belief in the old man's tirade began to show on some faces.

'Be silent!' thundered White Buffalo. 'Put an end to your wild talk!'

'It is too late for you to issue commands, White Buffalo-the-doubter,' shrilled the *shaman*. '*Look*!'

He swept a thin arm about him and a half-dozen young braves came running from the midst of the tepees at his back. All carried Winchester repeaters, two carried a box of the weapons between them and others had boxes of ammunition.

Eloise stifled a little screech of terror with her hand. Now she knew the secret of the cluster of trees close to the camp. Rifles had been cached there by the renegade whites, probably on the morning her brother had met the white man in the yellow slicker there, before the quarrel in which he was killed had flared up.

Big Tree had been plotting with other young men of the tribe that the ghost-dancing should commence at Spring River. She had known him to be carried away by old Owl's fanatical urgings and now her brother's fellow hotheads were rallying to the medicine-man with rifles.

The armed braves formed a protective ring around the gesticulating old medicine-man as White Buffalo advanced upon him.

'Lay down those weapons!' commanded the old chief. 'Nothing good can come of this — throw the rifles down!'

The armed bucks stood their ground around the medicine man, rifles pointed outwards, threatening their chief. Owl-in-the-Morning was leaping madly in the vivid glow of the flames.

'Your words have no power, White Buffalo! These men are following me now — they have paid heed to the prophesies of the chosen of the Great Spirit, Wovoka! The dances in preparation for the coming of the gods will commence at Spring River. The men of your tribe will join their brothers in the final, victorious fight against the white men who have plundered our hunting grounds and made false promises!' The old man emphasised his screeching with shrill blasts on his eagle-bone whistle and wild flourishes of his rattle.

Old White Buffalo moved closer to the group of rebels. His sub-chiefs left their places by the fire and hastened to his back.

'Throw down the rifles!' thundered the chief. 'I will not have my young men led into mischief by the foolish tongue of Owl-in-the-Morning!'

One of the braves, Small Dog, a surly and bad-tempered youngster, thrust the barrel of his rifle at White Buffalo's blanketed chest as the chief attempted to break through the ring of armed men. White Buffalo grasped the weapon in towering indignation, trying to force it aside. At that instant, Small Dog, with a face contorted in rage, fired.

Eloise screamed in unison with the crashing blast of the Winchester and the flash of muzzle-fire. As she rose to her feet, she saw the tall figure of her father go pitching backwards to the ground.

Then, hell was let loose around the camp fire. Another rifle barked and Six Bears, one of the sub-chiefs, crumpled down to the fire-painted earth. Rifle-butts were raised and slammed down over the heads of those loyal to their chief who rose to their feet to clash with the group of rebel fanatics. Sioux struggled with Sioux; squaws ran screaming, clutching their babies; dogs yapped around the feet of the frenzied, fighting Indians; children howled and, in the midst of the struggling mass of red-skinned humanity old Owl blew his eagle-bone whistle like a prancing demon.

Eloise wanted to rush to the prone body of her father, lying in the centre of the battling men, but found herself terror-rooted to the spot.

She stood on the fringe of the inferno of fire-lit, struggling activity, held her hands to her head and screamed again and again.

★ ★ ★

Out of Black Boulder and over the snow-blanketed plains rode Lance Costigan at dawn.

He had been the first to stir in the Dakota Palace, the first, that is, save for the Chinese cook who, sleep-eyed and yawning, prepared and served his breakfast.

The half-breed was well on his way to Lost Valley by the time the remaining guests at Black Boulder's hotel were astir, which was why he saw nothing of the obese, whiskered man or his blade-nosed, cold-eyed companion who had also spent the night there.

The wintry sweep of the sky was leaden with the promise of more snow and the chill-bladed wind whined keenly and ceaselessly over the wide prairie miles.

Costigan rode at a smart clip, yet not driving the horse too hard. When the sun was midway up the sky, splashing the land with a watery brilliance, he approached the timbered rim of Lost Valley. Setting the gelding at a walk, he rode cautiously down the valley side to the deep cover of a stand of aspen. From here, he could see the cabin, about three hundred yards below him. A feeble spiral of smoke, as though caused by someone just starting a fire, feathered up out of the stove-pipe. The smoke-stack of the still was dead. It was too early in the day for the production of rot-gut liquor to be under way, he decided.

Lance tethered the horse in the aspen grove, slithered his Winchester from its saddle-scabbard, unfastened his slicker so he could find easier access to his six-shooter.

As though in symbolism, he hefted

the .45 in its leather, then nudged it loose for easier clearance.

Crouching low, the half-breed cat-footed his way through the trees in the direction of the cabin, walking on the flat of his feet, Indian fashion. With his inborn Indian plains-savvy, he edged around the trees, positioning himself so that the wind would not carry his scent to the three saddled horses tethered at one side of the shack to scare them into whinnying.

The cabin made a tranquil picture. The new logs of the roof, showing where the snow had melted, contrasted with the older timber of the structure, moss grown with age. The feather of smoke wisped up from the rusted stove-pipe, grey against the background of snow-garlanded trees.

Costigan reached the cabin where one wall was pierced by a partly shattered and tiny window. Someone had stuffed a star-shaped hole in the grimy glass with an old cloth, but there was enough space left to allow

Lance a clear view of the interior of the log building when he pressed an eye to the glass for a brief instant.

He saw the warped figure of Eben Shaintuck seated at a rough wooden table with one of his young companions. Both had their backs to him. The third gun-runner was standing at the stove, also with his back to the window, puttering around with a coffee-pot. All three were attired simply in jeans and shirts. They wore no gun-gear and looked as though they had just rolled out of their bunks.

Lance darted away from the window and angled quickly around the shack towards the door.

It was going to be duck-soup! The men inside were totally unprepared for sudden intrusion.

There was a partially rusted latch on the door. Lance depressed it with a quick action of the hand and kicked the door open at the same time. He went in low, with the Winchester thrust before him. There was a tight, businesslike twist to his mouth.

'Hold everythin' right there!' he rasped harshly. 'Don't try any moves!'

Shaintuck and his companion at the table — Lance recognised him as the man he wanted most, the one with the Confederate buckle — half stood with a quick action like puppets worked by one string. At the same time, the one by the stove stiffened and turned slowly around. All three froze into still positions watching the half-breed with round eyes as though he was some peculiar object freshly dropped from the wide sky.

Eben Shaintuck found his voice first:

'What you want?' croaked the old-timer.

'All three of you, but mostly your friend with the CSA buckle on his belly — for murder.'

'You ain't no law-officer,' countered Shaintuck. 'You got no warrant for no arrests!'

'I'll tell you somethin' else I ain't,' mimicked Lance, in reply. 'I ain't foolin' an' I got no time for standin' here talkin'!'

Costigan swept his dark eyes around the shack. Three wooden bunks with tumbled blankets in them were affixed to the walls. A gun-belt with a six-gun in the holster was draped over one of the bunk-posts, close to the stove another set of gun-gear hung from a nail on the wall and a third was looped over the back of a chair fashioned from an old crate.

Lance moved into the cabin, leaving the door open behind him. He kept all three men under the sweep of his rifle barrel.

The three 'bad whites' watched him apprehensively.

'Move over here in a bunch,' Lance ordered. 'Stand together, shoulder-to-shoulder!'

The fellow over by the stove made a sudden sideways swoop, making for the gun-tackle hanging from the post of the nearby bunk. Lane swung the Winchester on to the man to counteract this move but, in doing so, he took his eyes from Shaintuck and his partner at the table. The oldster grabbed the edge of the table with the speed of a striking rattler and upended it towards the man with the Winchester. The table heeled over on its end and came crashing down on Costigan, showering him with an assortment of tin platters, cups, eating-irons and the contents of a freshly-opened can of beans.

Taken completely unaware by this speedy move, Lance sprawled back against the wall of the shack, still gripping the Winchester. He had a crazily whirling view of the youngster who had been going after the gun-gear coming at him through the chaos of scattered plates and cups, a six-shooter in his hand.

Lance fired the Winchester, hardly conscious of doing so. He saw the man go spinning backwards with his mouth wide open in a yell of agony. He hit the rusted stove-pipe and it snapped clean in two, then he slumped to the floor.

The slam of the rifle was still echoing round the narrow confines of the cabin.

Thick smoke was welling from the broken stove-pipe like blood from a slashed artery. Costigan crouched close to the overturned table. He could not see Shaintuck because of the dense gush of smoke, but was aware of the man with the Confederate buckle lunging through the haze with bunched fists, speedily, despite the bullet-crease Lance put in his side the day before. He kicked out at the table, between the man and himself, sending it slithering across the floor to hit the man he had come to think of as 'Yellow Slicker' in the region of the shins. This brought him floundering down over the fallen table to fall over Lance's body. Lance shoved him off with his free hand while a detached portion of his mind told him that he wanted this fellow alive, because of Big Tree's murder and the attack upon himself.

As Yellow Slicker sprawled gasping on

the floor, Costigan clubbed his Winchester and smote him over the back of the head with its butt. Yellow Slicker snorted into a still heap.

Then Eben Shaintuck was coming at him with a naked gun — the gun he had grabbed from the gear hanging on the wall.

At least, it looked as though the oldster was coming at him. The fact of the matter was that a slight clearing of the drift of smoke from the ruptured pipe revealed that Shaintuck had found the gun and, momentarily blinded by the acrid smoke, was searching for Costigan's whereabouts. He was spluttering and shaking his head and this gave Lance a chance to reverse the Winchester to a firing position.

'Don't try shootin,' Shaintuck!' he cautioned harshly.

Shaintuck shook his befuddled head again, then opened his old, red-rimmed eyes wide. Lance could see 'a killer's intention mirrored in them as Shaintuck levelled the gun at him.

He fired and the roar of the repeater merged with the bark of the old-timer's six-gun to form a bellowing explosion.

Lance threw himself down over the upturned table in the very act of triggering the Winchester. His hat had been lost somewhere in the earlier stages of the fracas and he felt the hot streak of the bullet from Shaintuck's gun zooming close to his scalp. The barking six-gun was near enough to him for the muzzle-fire to blind him for a moment.

Somewhere, off in another world, the *clump* of Shaintuck's bullet sounded as it bit into the wooden wall.

Costigan lay close to the unconscious form of Yellow Slicker, the upper part of his body propped up by the fallen table. He opened his cordite-stung eyes and with them saw Eben Shaintuck in the midst of the smoke-pall, gunless and beating the air feebly with his hands, as though fighting off invisible angry birds. All the time, he was sinking down through the drifts of smoke; like a man being slowly engulfed by quicksand. There was a red-edged hole in his chest.

He dropped suddenly as every muscle in his body was relaxed and he lay in a crumpled bundle, a death-rattle beginning in his throat.

Lance Costigan held his position for a minute, regaining his breath. Then, he was aware of a sighing grunt from somewhere near the stove. Through the swirl of wood-smoke, still spouting from the broken chimney-pipe, he saw the man he had shot first lying with a blood-running wound in his side, but still breathing and apparently unconscious.

The half-breed gathered himself up and crossed to the wounded man. His Winchester had inflicted a savage wound in his side, but the youngster stood a chance of recovering from that kind of injury, having youth and stamina on his side.

Costigan surveyed the shambles of

the cabin. Shaintuck sprawled dead as mutton; the unconscious Yellow Slicker over behind the upturned table; platters, cups and canned beans scattered over the floor and the broken stove-pipe gushing smoke into the room.

He told himself he had had a hell of a hectic few minutes and there was still that plant for the production of red-eye liquor, out in the newly-built annex to the cabin, waiting to be destroyed! There were supplies of rifles here, too, he felt, and wanted to find them.

The panicky whinny of one of the horses tethered outside the shack prompted him to hasten to the grimy, rag-stuffed window. Cautiously, he peered through the grubby glass.

He saw two riders on livery-stable plugs, black-clad men with the suggestion of the city about their heavy, square-cut coats, heading towards the cabin. One was fat and bewhiskered, the other tall with a blade of a nose and a gash of a mouth.

They were near. So near that Lance heard the lean one say quite plainly:

'Look at the smoke comin' from the doorway! Damn place must be on fire inside!'

7

Costigan looked quickly abut the smoke-filled cabin. The gun-runners, in repairing the original, caved-in roof, had supported it with four wide rafters, now half-hidden by the drifting smoke.

Lance shoved his Winchester under a blanket on one of the bunks, jumped slightly to grab one of the rafters and swung himself up to it. It was broad enough for him to lie flat along it with a good chance of evading detection from the smoky depths of the cabin. The half-breed drew his Colt and stretched his lean body along the rafter, arms held full-length in front of him.

He settled himself in position not a minute too soon. The two black-clad ones entered the room with loud exclamations of surprise.

Costigan could not see them from his position on the rafter, but heard their exchange of breathless remarks.

'Shaintuck's dead!' came a hard-edged voice. That would be the lean one, the obvious gunslinger. He recalled that Zeb Dockery had said he was Luke Quince, the South-Western gunman.

'Moate's caught it bad — shot in the side,' came the wheezy voice of the whiskered one. 'Who the hell did this, Luke? I didn't see any sign of anyone down here!'

Up on the rafter, Lance breathed an inaudible sigh of relief. That remark answered a question that had niggled at his mind ever since he first saw the approach of the pair; namely, whether they spotted his gelding tethered in the aspen grove. Seemingly, they had not and must have entered Lost Valley from some other route than the one he had used.

'Whoever did it has got clear away,' replied Quince, then, in a voice of quicker tempo, added: 'Say, Inskip ain't shot — just out cold!'

The staccato of a hand slapping the

123

senseless man's face came, accompanied by the voice of the black-clad ones urging the man to 'snap out of it'.

Eventually, their efforts were rewarded by a groan from Yellow Slicker, whose name, it seemed, was Inskip.

'What's been goin' on in here, Inskip?' asked the harsh voice of Quince.

Inskip muttered something inaudible for a time, then gathered his wits.

'Costigan, that damn half-breed!' he spluttered. 'He came in here with a gun, makin' talk about arrestin' me — we tried to roughhouse him. I guess he slugged me — '

'What was he tryin' to arrest you for?' It was the wheezy voice of the crooked lawyer that asked the question.

'He's workin' for the Army — lookin' out for trouble on the reservations. I had a ruckus out at Spring River an' a redskin got shot. I guess Costigan got wind of it an' pinned it down to us somehow. I dunno how he found out about this place, though.'

'Why didn't you three fix this Costigan galoot before this? It's a three to one proportion; you could've managed it quiet-like,' snorted Quince.

The man named Inskip grunted. 'I tried to ventilate him a coupla days ago an' he fought me off. I was hightailin' it from Spring River when I spotted him comin' over the prairie. I figured he was headed for the reservation an' didn't want him stickin' his nose in there just after the Injun was shot, so I holed up an' blasted at him — I missed!'

'You're a punk, Inskip,' snarled the voice of Quince. 'You're all talk an' brag, but when it comes to action, you can't even bushwhack a guy!'

A resentful noise came from Inskip.

'About this shootin' at Spring River,' put in Jethro Clute. 'How come the Indian was shot?'

'He was drunk! We were bargainin' about rifles an' he got ornery. Things got kinda heated between us an' he let fly at me. I ducked, but he plugged my horse. I had to shove my saddle on his

125

mustang right smart pronto an' hightail from the grove where we were bargainin'. I guess I just got clear of the reservation before the big trouble busted loose — the redskin was a chief's son!'

'He was drunk!' mimicked Clute. 'I figure he was drunk because you three were up to Shaintuck's old game — peddlin' booze on the side. Ain't that so?'

'Well, sure — but — ' began Inskip, hesitantly.

'Don't make excuses!' rasped Jethro Clute. 'When I sent you guys out here, there was no mention of red-eye in the plans. Shaintuck thought he'd cash in on that as a sideline. Well, look at the fix it put us in! Shaintuck's dead; Moate ain't got much of a chance from the way he looks, an' I feel like gunnin' you here an' now, Inskip. That'd be sufficient payment for the way you guys have bungled things out here!'

Lance Costigan, every nerve of his body tensed, lay on the rafter and listened to the exchange going on a few feet below his head. Here was proof indeed of the part played in the gun-running by the black-garbed pair who had arrived in the vicinity on the Bismarck coach, and he had learned something of the killing of Big Tree from the lips of the man who had committed the act. He held his position on the broad wooden beam, trigger-finger tensed.

The voice of Quince drifted up from the smoky room. 'I sure would admire to get the Costigan *hombre* on the business-end of my shootin'-iron — hey!' His voice, which drifted up from somewhere near the cabin door, broke off in a sudden yip of surprise. 'Hey! Let's get out of here — here comes the Army!'

There came a muttered curse and a scuffling of feet as the two other men hastened to the door. The voice of Inskip came up through the smoke, jittery:

'A blue-coat patrol! They're just

comin' over the valley rim. Let's run for it. We better pick up Ed Moate an' get him over his horse.'

'To hell with Moate,' growled Quince. 'If I'm runnin' from the Army, I ain't luggin' no half-dead *hombre* with me. Leave him here!'

From his hiding place, Lance heard the scuffle of boots running from the cabin. So they'd left their dying comrade, he thought grimly.

Speedily, he swung down from the rafter and hastened to the door, the Colt gripped in his hand in a businesslike fashion. From the door, he could see a straggle of distance-tiny blue-attired riders coming down the glaring whiteness of the snow-carpeted valley slope. From the side of the cabin, he heard a whoop, followed by the drumming of departing hoofs. He remembered that there would be two more horses tethered around there, Eben Shaintuck's and Moate's.

He ran through the door and raced round to the side of the structure.

Clute, Quince and Inskip were loping away in a bobbing trio, Inskip mounted on a saddle-less horse.

Hope of pursuing them died in Lance's breast when he reached the spot where the gun-runners had tethered their horses, for the fleeing trio had turned the remaining two horses loose and they were hazing off in another direction, scared by the thundering approach of the mounted soldiers, now drawing closer.

Lance cursed and loosed a slug after the riding men. It was wide, but the report of his six-gun caused them to turn around. Quince's voice sounded thinly on a surprised note:

'It's Costigan, by grab!' From under his black, square-cut coat, his revolver came up in a glittering arc. He fired as he spurred his horse onward and, in spite of the ever-increasing range, the slug came whanging close to Lance's head.

Lance ducked to one side and replied with a calculated shot. To his own surprise, he heard a squeak of pain as the bullet winged Quince in the arm. He saw the lean, black rider clutch at the wound and his angry voice came echoing thinly along the valley just before he and his companions disappeared over a hump.

'I'll get you one day, Costigan!'

'If I don't get you first!' replied the half-breed at the top of his lungs.

He cursed the fact that his own horse was tethered in the grove so far up the valley side. With the gelding under him he could ride after the gun-runners with a flaming Colt. As it was, they had a clear run along the far side of the valley, making for who-knew-where.

At length, the little squad of cavalrymen came pounding up with a jingle of trappings. There were about a dozen, led by old Sergeant Zeb Dockery.

They pulled their horses to a halt at a hand signal from Dockery.

'The major's been plumb worried

about you, Lance,' called the grizzled old non-com. 'He sent us to look for you. When I gave him your letter, he said he figured you were plumb foolish to go stickin' your nose into a hornet's nest like this on your lonesome!'

'Don't worry none about me,' rapped Lance. 'Get after those guys — they're gettin' clear away!'

'We'll have to catch 'em another day, Lance,' retorted Zeb Dockery with a shake of his head. 'We have to join the rest of the column over at Spring River. You'd better come, too!'

'Spring River! What's happening over there?'

'All hell's let loose! A crowd of fanatics under old Owl-in-the-Morning has taken control an' they've got guns. Old White Buffalo has been killed!'

'White Buffalo dead!' echoed Costigan. A chilly horror gripped him at the thought that Eloise might have been harmed.

So the bubble had finally burst, he thought. The half-crazed medicine-man had gained control at Spring River and the last thing that any sane man, Indian or white, wanted to see was sure to happen — the killing of red men and white would break out again in the same old senseless way.

'Let me get my cayuse from up thc valley-side an' I'll ride with you,' Lance told the old sergeant. He suddenly remembered the wounded man, Moate, lying in the cabin. 'There's a man there lyin' wounded. One of the gun-runnin' crowd. Maybe you can detail a couple of men to take care of him an' take him to Fort Yates as a prisoner, Zeb. They can also destroy the whiskey still in the little lean-to at the side of the cabin an' they might find rifles stored somewhere in the shack.'

'Sure,' agreed the Sergeant. 'Now you better get that hoss of yourn an' ride with us. You'll be a mighty helpful man in parlyin' with the Indians.'

Lance nodded absently and made off in the direction of the aspen grove where he had left his gelding. His thoughts were full of the slender, bronzed girl who had kissed him that day in the snowstorm. If anything had happened to Eloise, he'd —

Well, somebody would get hurt!

8

As they rode for Spring River, Zeb
Dockery told Lance something of what
had happened at the reservation.

It seemed that one of the assistant
storekeepers from the Spring River
Agency had come riding into Fort
Yates, more dead than alive. He had
managed to escape after being shot
when a bunch of crazy young bucks
swooped on the reservation headquarters, killing all the whites.

He had watched for his chance,
managed to jump a horse and ride clear
away from the scene of the violent
outbreak.

To Major Aitchison, he told a grim
story. The armed followers of old Owl,
many of them drunk, were holding
White Buffalo's camp in a grip of
terror. The ghost-dancing had already
broken out, many of the Indians, still

loyal to the restraining ideals of White Buffalo being forced to dance at rifle-point. Owl-in-the-Morning and his fanatics were threatening death to all who showed any resistance. The fierce savagery of the Sioux was rampant and the scene at the camp was one such as had not been witnessed since the Indian wars of nearly twenty years before. Major Aitchison had taken a column out at once, complete with a Gatling gun.

Apparently, he was still seething at what he considered to be a madcap action — Lance's venture into Lost Valley alone. On the way to Spring River, he detailed Dockery and his small patrol to enter the valley half-expecting that they would find the half-breed had fallen victim to the 'bad whites'.

Lance listened to the old sergeant's tale with a pounding heart. Overriding all other thoughts, was the nagging worry that some harm had come to Eloise. He knew she would never voluntarily join the followers of the old *shaman*. He knew also that Owl-in-the-Morning was the bitter enemy of White Buffalo. With White Buffalo dead the half-insane wizard might kill Eloise simply because she was the daughter of his old enemy, the chief.

He rode to the fore of the galloping patrol, his mount keeping pace with that of Zeb Dockery. It seemed an eternity of hard riding to the jangle of accoutrements before they hit Spring River Agency land. From somewhere in the distance came the angry crackle of firing, making his heart leap.

'That's at White Buffalo's camp,' grunted Dockery. 'Sounds like our boys have clashed with the redskins. The Major sorta hoped the sight of uniforms an' a Gatlin' would make them throw their hand in without any more trouble.'

'They're givin' trouble all right,' retorted Lance, grimly. 'When a Sioux gets down to fightin' it usually takes a lot of persuasion to make him lay off.

By the continuous sound of that fire, I'd say they were exchanging shots in good and earnest!'

The patrol came drumming down to the creek bottom at a brisk tattoo. Gunsmoke drifted over the tepees of White Buffalo's camp, on the opposite side of the creek, in a heavy pall. Soldiers were under cover on all sides of the cluster of Indian lodges and down at the creek side, exchanging rifle shots with Sioux who were firing from the camp perimeter. A Gatling was assembled on a rise, its revolving barrels directed at the centre of the cluster of tepees.

Sergeant Dockery's patrol pulled rein in a clearing in a stand of pine in which Major Aitchison and two junior officers stood on the snow, surveying the scene with a West Point straightness to their backs and sour expressions on their faces.

Dockery saluted, and reported that he had found Costigan and detailed two men to care for and take under arrest the wounded gun-runner.

Major Aitchison was a stern-faced man with a moustache and beard modelled on those of General George A. Custer, who still commanded some hero-worship among officers of the cavalry. He fixed Lance with a hard eye.

'Costigan, you were a fool to go into that valley alone. Why didn't you wait for some support from me? A patrol could have attended to the bad whites in there if you'd waited for me to send one. I thought my men were sure to find you dead!'

'I figured makin' a grab for the birds while they were in the bush was the best way of handlin' the chore, Major,' Lance replied. 'I killed one an' shot another up bad, but three more, includin' two of the men who're pullin' the strings got away. I was able to confirm, at least, that the men I wrote you about — the lawyer and Quince, the gunfighter — are big men in the gun-runnin' game. The fellows in the cabin at Lost Valley were merely their agents out here.'

'You can make an official report on the Lost Valley business later, Costigan. Meantime, we have big trouble on our hands right here. Hear that!' He jerked his wide-brimmed hat in the direction of the camp. A frenzied, guttural chanting was rising up from the midst of the tepees.

It was the same chant Lance had heard at Standing Rock and Pine Ridge, where the ghost-dancing had broken out months before.

'That's one of the ghost-chants,' Costigan said.

'Yes,' replied the officer. 'That maniac of a medicine-man has whipped them up into a frenzy and the ghost-dancing is going on full swing. The difference here is that the Indians are armed and the redskins are worked up to a pitch where they'll pay no attention to old Wovoka's original prophesy that the dancing must continue without harm to the whites — these Indians will kill!'

Lance canted his head towards the

threatening Gatling. 'Do you intend usin' that?' he asked.

'Not unless I have to,' the officer replied. 'All attempts to parley have failed. That old Owl-in-the-Morning has the place in his grip and he seems to have plenty of power!'

'Only among the drunken bucks who are lookin' for trouble,' the half-breed said. 'There are peaceful Indians in there and women and kids!'

The officer stared at Lance, with the realisation that he had an allegiance to white and red men.

'I'll have to use that Gatling, Costigan, if they don't throw down their arms and come out as my prisoners pretty soon. The main ones I want are old Owl and the young bucks with the rifles. One burst of Gatling fire over the top of the tepees might be sufficient to scare them into submission.'

'It's too risky!' Lance was thinking of Eloise somewhere in the midst of the camp — but was she alive or dead? 'It's too risky, Major. I don't want to see women an' kids killed by Gatling fire!'

'Neither do I, Costigan, but my job is to prevent an Indian rising — one way or the other! Old Owl refuses to listen to our parleying, so we'll probably have to smoke them out sooner or later. This armed defiance could be the spark that would set the whole of the Sioux nation on the warpath if it spread to the other reservations. I can't risk that!'

'Then let me parley with them. They understand me an' respect me to some extent.'

'You can try,' the officer replied. 'Our attempts to make talk have failed so far, but you can try.'

Lance walked down to where a trio of blue-coated soldiers squatted behind a clump of brush beside the creek, carbines at the ready. From the perimeter of the nearby Indian encampment, a wild shot whanged out in his direction. He streaked out his six-gun as he ducked low from the flying bullet and sprinted the last few yards to where

141

the soldiers were positioned.

'What sort of opposition you gettin' here?' he inquired as he threw himself down with the cavalrymen.

'Not heavy,' grunted one of the blue-coats. 'The only redskin who's givin' us much trouble is the one who fired at you just now. He's holed up behind one of the lodges with a Winchester. I guess he's had his fill of firewater — but he can shoot almighty well. We three have been tryin' to pick him off for half-an-hour. Most of the others have sobered down some on account of the Gatlin' gun lookin' right at 'em the way it is!'

'Cover me,' ordered Lance. 'I'm goin' to mosey down to the tepees an' try talkin' some sense into them. Look out for the brave you just told me about, but if he shows no signs of fight, don't shoot.'

Cautiously, with his Colt gripped in his hand, he left the brush and angled off towards the cluster of tents, half-crouching, but moving speedily. He waded through a part of the creek where the icy water was only knee-deep.

He could see paint-daubed faces regarding him impassively from positions among the tepees; the Sioux who were too frightened of the threatening Gatling to fire.

From behind one lodge, however, a hate-contorted copper face showed itself and the wintry sun touched a silver sheen on the bright barrel of a brand-new Winchester. At this distance, Costigan could recognise the features as those of Small Dog, whom he knew to be a bitter malcontent.

Small Dog was in the act of throwing the Winchester butt to his naked shoulder, but Lance raised his free hand in the Indian greeting of peace.

'No, Small Dog!' he roared in the Sioux tongue and he kept up his crouching advance. 'I come to make talk with the Sioux!'

He was very close to the perimeter of the camp now. He saw Small Dog lower the rifle a little uncertainly, then the Indian called:

'He who is the son of a Sioux mother and a white father comes with one hand holding a gun and the other in the sign of peace. Which hand is Small Dog to heed?' Small Dog was very drunk.

Lance hesitated. He could see the foolish expression on the face of the Indian — the expression brought by indulgence in whiskey. The half-breed knew he was taking a big risk, but he replaced his Colt in its leather.

He was standing upright now and walking slowly towards the tents of the Sioux camp. Small Dog emerged fully into the open. He was standing only a matter of yards away from Lance, rifle hanging limply down.

'Heed the hand of peaceful greeting, Small Dog!' he shouted, throwing up his right hand in the gesture that indicated peaceful intentions. 'Tell your brothers to throw down their guns. Only death can come from this defiance of the Great White Father's blue-coats! They stand ready with the big gun that spins and speaks quick death. The Sioux have no chance against its powerful medicine!'

There was a tense and heart-pounding moment during which both men stood staring one at the other. Small Dog lurched drunkenly for an instant. Then, he grinned a foolish, drunken Indian's grin.

'You are a fool!' he yelled and threw the rifle to his shoulder. Lance pitched himself into a gunfighter's crouch, clawing for his gun as he went.

It came up, spitting red flame in a streaking arc and the bullet slammed into Small Dog's naked chest as he was in the act of triggering the repeater. The bullet from the smuggled weapon ploughed a furrow on the snow at his feet as he toppled over backwards to the accompaniment of the carbine shots which the soldiers covering Lance fired on the heels of his six-gun song.

One of the cavalrymen behind the

clump of brush whistled a low indication of surprise.

'Look at what he's doin' now! He's runnin' forward into the camp — he'll be killed for sure!'

The soldiers, expecting Costigan to return to cover after his failure to 'make talk', watched him, six-shooter still in hand, run forward, haring for the midst of the lodges.

Lance realised he was taking his life into his hands by going through with this action, but he had a notion that, if he could find Owl-in-the-Morning and somehow drag the old mischief-maker out to Major Aitchison, the loss of their leader might well cause the remaining malcontents to give up their armed defiance. Besides, he wanted to find Eloise!

From behind a tepee came two painted, coppery bodies flourishing rifles, running to intercept the half-breed as he entered the camp.

Lance converted his crouching run into a forward dive through the air and butted the first one heavily in the midriff. The Sioux teetered backwards with a screech and fell to the snow with Lance sprawling atop him.

Costigan slammed the barrel of his Colt down over the red man's head, to knock him senseless.

He twisted his body about and saw the remaining Indian standing over him, rifle clubbed and raised. He kicked his feet upwards, took the Indian's legs from under him with a powerful thrusting kick. The Sioux scooted backwards in the snow, then lost his balance and fell flat on his back on the ground. Lance gathered himself into a bundle and sprang forward to land on the fallen Indian. They rolled, threshing and kicking in the crisp snow, the Indian clawing wildly and drunkenly about for the Winchester he had dropped.

Lance managed to pin the naked, copper-hued shoulders to the ground and cracked a hard fist of knuckles across the redskin's jaw, reducing him to a still heap.

He picked up the Winchester, 'broke' it and emptied the magazine of its shells. These, he kicked far and wide over the snow, and treated the shells from the carbine of the first Indian he had quelled in a similar fashion. He retrieved his Colt from where he had dropped it during the scuffle with the second Sioux, ever-watching for sign of further opposition.

He stiffened suddenly at the sight of two feathered heads showing from around the edge of a buffalo-hide lodge, then relaxed his lean features into a grin.

These two Sioux, lying flat on the ground and clutching repeaters, had fallen victim to the fate that usually overtook drunken Indians. Far from offering fight, they were sound asleep!

One of the prone red men was wearing a buffalo-robe which Lance, after rendering their repeaters useless, snatched up and draped around his shoulders. He snatched the feathered head-dress from the greasy hair of one of the sleeping Sioux and arranged it on his own black locks. Keeping his head down and the Colt ready under the buffalo-robe, he moved into the midst of the straggle of Indian lodges.

His half-breed features, buffalo-robe and head-feathers made him look enough like an Indian to pass at a first glance, but he hoped the cowboy boots, showing below the robe, went unnoticed long enough for him to carry out the plan he had in mind.

From the centre of the camp, the high-pitched chants of the ghost-dance rituals came throbbing out. Costigan kept close to the lodges and moved cautiously with head down. He passed one or two drowsy-looking Sioux who were obviously drunk and paid little attention to him. He reflected that the number of tipsy redskins in the camp, showed to what extent the rot-gut whiskey, distilled by Eben Shaintuck and his partners, had been smuggled into the reservation with the connivance of Joe Folinsbee.

At length, his stealthy progression brought him to the main clearing in the arrangements of the camp. He stood close to the skin wall of a lodge and took in the scene of wild activity.

A fire smouldered in the middle of the clearing. Around it, in a slowly moving circle, like sleepwalkers, moved a group of ghost-dancers. Lance had seen the dances before, over at Standing Rock and Pine Ridge. The pattern here was the same. The braves and squaws who were dancing must have been at it for hours. They now moved mechanically, almost ready to drop from exhaustion, but managing to put one foot before the other. Some had already collapsed and their limp bodies had been dragged to one side of the slowly moving circle of dancers. A circle of chanters, also carried away into a half-dream world by the hypnotic rhythms of the rituals, squatted in the background.

Lance knew that this shuffling dancing and wild, toneless chanting had gone on for days on the other reservations, with fresh dancers and singers taking the places of those who fell asleep or collapsed from sheer physical exhaustion. More than one death had resulted from the frenzied rituals. The Indians were not overfed by the whites who had charge of issuing rations and, in such a condition, even the traditionally stoical redskin was unable to carry out the dancing without suffering physical harm.

Costigan's dark eyes flashed around the clearing. There were a number of young bucks, drunken-looking and flourishing rifles at one side. They were obviously keeping their eyes on some of the older men and women of the camp who squatted in surly silence. Lance knew most of them, all were of the type likely to remain loyal to old White Buffalo. Old Owl-in-the-Morning was making his presence felt at the perimeter of the zombie-like dancers circling the campfire. His scrawny figure was leaping around in a fanatical fashion.

The keening of his eagle-bone whistle and the dry cackle of his wizard's rattle alternated against the colourless background of the chanting. Occasionally, the sporadic crackle of firing echoed from where the Sioux held off Major Aitchison's men. Lance could see no sign of Eloise as he stood watching the fantastic scene of the ghost-dance ritual.

The thought that she might now be dead was a cold needle stabbing deep into his mind. He had to find her, just as he had to break old Owl's madman's hold on the people of White Buffalo.

He squatted in the lee of the lodge, holding his head down, simulating the posture of a drunken brave and watching the old medicine-man. Old Owl-in-the-Morning was some ten yards away, close to the dancers, carrying out his whooping, whistle-blowing routine. Every once in a while he made a leap into the air, each leap bringing him down a little closer to where the disguised half-breed crouched.

Lance watched the old *shaman's*

maddenly slow progression with sharp and calculating eyes.

Slowly, the whooping, leaping old man in the tattered buffalo-robe moved closer. The chanting and the weary shuffling of moccasins, spiced with the distant exchange of fire, was a tension-edged theme song to the jittery apprehension that niggled at Lance Costigan's unconsciousness.

He waited, tensed.

Then, there were only a few yards separating him from the old medicine-man. He crouched down, like a sprinter preparing for the starter's pistol — and he started to hare across the clearing at a dead-run, the buffalo-robe flapping in the breeze as he went. Under the robe, he clutched his Colt, finger hooked around the trigger.

His sudden, wild arrival was a complete surprise to the Sioux in the camp fire clearing and he took old Owl unawares. He streaked up behind the old man while he was preparing for one of his frenzied leaps, threw the encumbering buffalo-robe from about his shoulders and grabbed Owl with a sinewy arm crooked about the old wizard's scrawny neck. He held him tight, ramming the mouth of his Colt into his back.

With a raspy squawk, Owl-in-the-Morning dropped his rattle and whistle.

A surprised yell and a flourish of guns came from the drunken braves in the clearing. The dancers, in their hypnotised fashion, continued to shuffle round the fire like moving dead.

'Don't move — anybody!' yelled Lance, in the Sioux dialect. 'If anyone tries to shoot, your brother Owl-in-the-Morning, who is a foolish man to bring the wrath of the White Father's blue-coats upon you, will die!'

The braves with the rifles froze into stillness, realising the half-breed had a gun planted firmly in the medicine-man's' back.

Old Owl uttered a gurgle in the Sioux tongue: 'He has a gun at my back!'

Lance tightened his grip on the old man's stringy neck. He could feel the old frame shaking with fear under his grip. The bucks with rifles were standing in wide-eyed uncertainty.

'You heard the old man,' Costigan shouted. 'I have a gun in his bony old back! One move from any of you and I shoot him dead!'

Owl-in-the-Morning gurgled another dry squawk which served to emphasise the half-breed's threat. Lance put his lips close to the medicine-man's ear and whispered:

'The woman, Sun-on-Water, where is she?'

No reply. Costigan jabbed the revolver into the old Indian's back impatiently. 'The daughter of White Buffalo, you old carrion-crow! Where is she?'

Mentally, he swore that, if Eloise was dead, he would shoot this old upstart of a fanatic here and now.

'In the lodge of her father,' rasped the old medicine-man, with difficulty. 'She is in her father's lodge — unharmed!'

He was thoroughly cowed and Lance turned his obvious fear to his own account. In a voice heavy with scorn, he roared to the armed braves:

'Behold Owl-in-the-Morning now, my brothers! This is the man who used his twisted tongue to incite you to defy the law of the white man, now you see him as a coward!'

The half-breed kept up a barrage of talk in this vein while he moved slowly backwards, dragging old Owl with him. He knew White Buffalo's lodge lay some little distance at his back. He kept the mouth of the six-gun rammed firmly against the old Indian's back.

Mob-oratory went a long way with Indians, he knew, and he scolded the Sioux loudly as he cat-footed backwards, keeping the corner of his eye alert for the decorated lodge-pole of White Buffalo's dwelling. The rot-gut liquor the Indians had so lately imbibed served to increase their gullibility and Lance could see he was swaying them with his talk.

'You are fools to follow the lead of old Owl!' he shouted to them. 'Can you not see he is a power-mad fool? His talk of the ghost-gods is the idle talk of one who has not the welfare of his brothers at heart. If you followed the wisdom of your chief, White Buffalo, you would still be at peace; instead, White Buffalo and his son, Big Tree, are dead and you are surrounded by blue-coats with powerful weapons — because of this old fool's crazy talk!'

Murmurings and grunts of half-approval issued from some of the Indians and the wizened old *shaman* was dithering visibly in Lance's grip.

Costigan cast a quick glance over his shoulder, saw he was close to White Buffalo's lodge, flung Owl-in-the-Morning from him and ran for the lodge.

A babble of excited Sioux sounded in his wake as he gained the opening of the skin structure. It sounded as though the Indians were squabbling among themselves, some wanting to attack the old medicine-man. Lance felt no sympathy for Owl. Any fate that overtook him now would be payment for the machinations of his crafty mind which had brought the Sioux of White Buffalo to their present straits.

The interior of the dead chief's lodge was gloomy, but Lance saw Eloise, a dejected little figure, sitting close to the central lodge-pole.

She gasped when she saw him come through the aperture, gun in hand. He was an unusual figure in his range-rider's garb and Indian warrior head-dress, which still adorned his jet-black hair.

The Indian girl rose to her feet quickly, rushed to him and clutched his sleeve.

'Lance!' she gasped. 'Oh, Lance, it's terrible. Half the camp is following old Owl and my father is dead — !'

'Who killed your father?' he asked, cutting in on her sentence. He realised that, somewhere, was the murderer who had shot his old friend the chief. He was filled with a sudden and over-whelming desire to seek out that Indian and punish him.

'Small Dog,' Eloise replied.

'Small Dog?' he echoed. 'Then your father's murderer is dead; Small Dog was killed a few minutes back.'

Costigan grabbed the girl around her slender waist and pulled her towards the door of the lodge.

'C'mon, we must get out of here. I've discredited old Owl somewhat in front of the rest of the camp, but I don't know how the feelin' is runnin' out there!'

Cautiously, gun at the ready, he pushed his nose outside the door of the chief's lodge.

Outside, a commotion was going on with the wildly gesticulating figure of Owl-in-the-Morning at its centre. From drifts of the babbled Sioux that Lance heard, he gathered the feelings concerning the old medicine-man were mixed. In the background the shuffling ghost-dance and the chanting continued.

Costigan edged out of the lodge, taking the girl with him. One of the drunken young braves who was still loyal to the medicine-man loosed a wild whoop and two sinewy red bodies came running towards Lance and Eloise.

'Run for the edge of the camp!' Lance urged the girl. They began to run as though all the demons of hell were on their tails, two tipsy Indians, whooping and lurching after them.

Without warning, a sudden series of deafening explosions began to stutter out. Glancing over his shoulder, Lance saw a tepee collapse under a blow like that of a steam-hammer. Yells of agony sounded out of a chaos of sound behind the running pair and one of the pursuing redskins fell kicking to the ground, making the snow crimson with his blood.

Lance Costigan swore lustily as he ran beside the daughter of White Buffalo.

'Keep running, Eloise,' he gasped. 'That fool Aitchison has opened up with a Gatling gun!'

9

Running as fast as their legs would carry them and gasping for breath, Eloise and Lance broke through the cluster of tepees on the creek bottom. Behind them reigned fear-fraught activity. Sioux were running on all sides to escape the rain of Gatling-gun shots descending on the camp. The air was filled with screams of women and children, the hoarse yelling of men, the panicky yapping of the camp curs and, overriding all was the bellowing stutter of the Gatling-gun.

Skin tepees were overturned as they were struck by the devastating shots. Indians lay in the snow, some kicking in pain, others ominously still.

Costigan was cursing loudly as he and the girl broke through the perimeter of the camp on the far side of where the stuttering Gatling was positioned.

Major Aitchison was a fool. Something had panicked him into ordering the Gatling to be fired. Welling up in Lance was a blind and all-consuming fury against the cavalry officer. He realised now, more than at any time before, that he belonged to the Sioux as much as he did the whites. The sight of the Indians who had been led astray by a foolish and power-hungry medicine-man, being mown down by one of the most deadly field-pieces of the time sparked off a half-mad rage within him. If it had not been for the connivance of the 'bad whites', with their gun- and whiskey smuggling, the chances of old Owl-in-the-Morning gaining the upper hand would have been very slight. Now, White Buffalo's Sioux, many of whom were still loyal to their dead chief's ideals, were being mown down in their camp.

The half-breed and the Indian girl emerged from the camp at a point close to the creek. Eloise dropped to the long grass that spiked through the snow at

162

the water's edge, fighting for her breath. Lance squatted beside her, panting.

At their backs, in the midst of the camp, the sounds of screaming Indians still rent the thin wintry air against the loud, pounding explosions of the Gatling.

'Eloise, stay here!' Costigan ordered the girl. 'I have to stop those fool soldiers from killin' everyone in the camp! You're quite safe here, you're well out of the Gatling's range. I'm goin' across the creek an' I'll try to stop that gun — they're murderin' women an' children!'

The girl, sitting on the snow-crusted grass in her simple buckskin dress, her dark eyes wide and wisps of her raven hair straggling about her copper-skinned face, looked like a frightened and hounded wild thing. To Lance Costigan, she was suddenly a symbol of all the plains Indians. Hunted by whites; herded on to reservations to be robbed of the age-old, free-roaming way of life that had always been theirs;

called savages and butchers simply because they had fought back against the land-grasping, 'civilising' whites in defence of their homes.

This time, it was Costigan who did the kissing. He knelt close to the Sioux girl, gathered her in his arms and kissed her long and hungrily.

The Gatling pounded in the background and the children of wise old White Buffalo, who had ruled his people in peace for so long, screamed and scurried about in blind panic.

'Stay here — I'll be back!' sad Lance tersely. Then he was on his feet and making for the snow-swollen creek.

He waded into the strong current until the water was close to his waist and threatening his holstered six-gun and cartridge-belt, He halted for a moment and unbuckled these then continued wading through the icy water with the gun-gear held over his head.

In midstream, the water was almost to his chest and the current so strong as to almost buffet him off his feet. He kept moving, surprising himself with the speed he was making, urged on by the pulsing hatred of the loudly blasting Gatling on the other side of the creek.

Panting, and with his wet and chilled clothing clinging to his body, he reached the other side of the creek. Pausing only to buckle his gun-gear about him, he set off, angling away towards the position of the Gatling-gun, the water squelching in his boots as he went.

Costigan burst into the main concentration of Major Aitchison's troops like a madman.

Up on the knoll, the field-piece, with its revolving barrels whirling, was slamming its rapid shots into the heart of the Indian encampment across the water. The blue-coats manning the weapon were actually grinning through the thick haze of the Gatling's smoke.

'Damn them!' thought Lance, half-crazed. '*They're enjoyin' it*!'

He slogged forward in the direction of the gun, not knowing what he intended to do. Major Aitchison, his two West Point-stiffened young officers trailing in his wake, intercepted him.

'Costigan! Where have you been? We thought you dead. We thought those savages — '

'I could've been dead — I could've been cut to shreds by the damn Gatling!' Lance's voice was almost a snarl, cutting the officer short in mid-sentence. 'I could've been killed like the defenceless squaws and children in that camp. Order them to stop firing, Major!'

Aitchison stood his ground stiffly, regarding Costigan down his nose. 'Costigan, I decided the armed resistance from the camp had gone far enough. The only way to quell savages is to show them a strong hand!'

Lance stood with his legs wide apart, his whole body in its water-sogged clothing quivering with rage. His lips were drawn wide apart and he spoke through clenched teeth.

'Major Aitchison, you forget that half

of me belongs to these people you call *savages*! Those human beings across the creek have been led astray by a half-crazy wizard with the help of whites as full-blooded as yourself. Most of them are still true to their old chief an' I've talked the nonsense out of the majority of them an' they're ready to give up. *But your men are slaughtering them!*'

'You seem to forget I'm in command here,' retorted the Major

From the corner of his eye, Lance could see the grove in which he had tethered his gelding when he arrived with Dockery's patrol. A wild plan formed in his mind.

'I don't care if President Harrison himself is in command,' he grated through clenched teeth. 'I'm stopping that Gatling-gun!'

He swivelled on his heel and began to run for the grove.

'Costigan!' bellowed Aitchison, red in the face.

'Go to hell, Major,' came the retort

over the running man's shoulder.

Running up the slight rise that gave on to the grove where his horse was tethered, Lance had a glimpse of the officer and his straight-backed juniors standing open-mouthed, making a tableau of surprised indignation. He told himself he didn't care for them, any of them and to blazes with the consequences of his back-chatting the Major. He was working for the Army, but he was no soldier, and he figured he was right in his argument against Aitchison's bull-headed action.

In the grove, he found his gelding cropping grass that showed in sparse patches through half-melted snow. His range-riding gear was still at the saddle, with the exception of his Winchester. That was where he had left it, in the cabin at Lost Valley.

Down the drift, the gunners had paused to reload the Gatling. He could see them bobbing about the field-piece in a haze of smoke. He swung into the saddle just as the staccato clatter of the gun opened up again.

With a savage action, he snatched his lariat from the saddle-horn and touched his spurs deep into the gelding's hide.

The animal went out of the trees at a smart clip, as though stung by a swarm of hornets and he rowelled his spurs even deeper.

Aitchison, his young officers and a cluster of blue-coats scattered as they saw him come pounding out of the grove, a wild, bareheaded horseman riding with his head low over the gelding's back and swinging his lariat.

Costigan headed the horse up the knoll on which the Gatling was mounted, headed straight for the weapon. He held the rope at the ready, as though out to catch a hazing maverick at round-up time, until he topped the knoll. Then he angled off almost in the very face of the blasting weapon, slinging an expert wide-loop over its revolving, death spitting ordnance and, yipping in frenzied cowboy fashion to cause the gelding to lope off

169

at full speed, yanked hard on the lariat.

The lassoed Gatling went toppling over, broadside on, its wheels spinning madly and the soldiers who had been operating it tumbling about in a cursing tangle.

Major Aitchison watched the half-breed's saddle-jogged figure with whiskers positively bristling.

'The renegade!' he growled. 'I — I'll have him before a court for this!' The officer was shuffling about in anger, almost performing a war-dance in the snow.

'Look at him now, sir,' pointed out one of the beardless junior officers. 'He's riding on down the hill, dragging the gun with him.' With eyes almost popping from his head, Aitchison watched the wildly riding figure, long hair streaming in the breeze, pulling the roped gun with him in a plume of disturbed snow as he came down the knoll. After dragging the Gatling for several yards, Lance released his grip on the rope and the weapon was left upturned in the snow, a broken wheel spinning slowly. Up on the knoll, a corporal and his squad of gunners were picking themselves up and howling colourful opinions after the riding half-breed.

Lance slowed his gelding to a walk, wheeled the animal and rode slowly back to the officers. His coal-black eyes were flashing and there was a determined set to his jaw as he approached.

'I'll clap him in irons,' thundered Major Aitchison into his Custer-like beard. 'I'll make sure he doesn't see daylight for months!'

Lance tightened his rein to halt the horse facing the officer. 'The cost of the damage to the Gatlin' can be taken from my pay, Major Aitchison,' he said coldly without dismounting. 'I'm quittin' as an Army agent here an' now — I don't want any part of anythin' brought on by fools like you. Your kind causes Indian trouble because you're too damn hamfisted to use any method but brute-force — an' you have the nerve to refer to those Sioux across the creek as *savages*! I'm goin' after the men who had most to do with stirrin' up this trouble, the renegade whites who got away at Lost Valley. But, I'm goin' after them on my own account — not the Army's!'

Aitchison stood spread-legged in the snow, his bewhiskered features running through various shades of red.

'You all-fired fool, Costigan,' blurted he. 'Do you think I'm going to let you get away with what you've just done? I'm having you packed back to Fort Yates in irons!'

Lance Costigan was not listening to the officer. He was staring across the creek towards the perimeter of the Indian encampment. A group of braves, led by old Owl-in-the-Morning, was coming dejectedly out of the shambles of the tepees that had tumbled under the fire of the Gatling. Some of them were injured and all held their hands up in gestures of submission. To Costigan, there was something pitiful about the sight, although he knew the redskins had, to some extent, brought their troubles upon themselves. They were basically a childlike people and they had fallen for the wild talk of old Owl, while men like Shaintuck and Folinsbee, who had no loyalty to even their own kind, took the red men's meagre money in exchange for the forbidden rifles and whiskey.

To Lance, there was something symbolic and saddening about the little band of surrendering Sioux. The once proud warriors of the plains, coming out of their wrecked village weaponless and with hands held high, giving themselves as prisoners to the bluecoats.

'They're givin' themselves up, Major Aitchison,' he said icily. 'There's no fight left in them any more. There wasn't any real fight in them, just booze an' foolish words! This whole trouble could've been settled without a Gatling-gun!'

Aitchison jerked his head in the

direction of the party of Sioux. 'Take a party across the creek and attend to those Indians, Briggs,' he ordered one of the younger officers at his side. Then he added, to the second lieutenant: 'Put Costigan under arrest, Soames!'

The youngster relaxed his West Point stiffness and came moving towards Lance, his hand wandering in the direction of the Colt holstered at his shiny belt.

Neither he nor his superior officer saw the mounted half-breed's hand move. It was suddenly a blur, streaking towards his holster then it stilled, holding a Colt .45 levelled at the head of Lieutenant Soames.

'Don't try pullin' that gun, sonny,' he warned the young Army man. 'I don't intend to let myself be slapped into irons in some Army guardhouse while the galoots I want to even up with get clear away. If I act fast, I have a chance of catching up with them.'

The young officer had guts. He went through with the draw in the face of

Costigan's naked gun.

The army model Colt came up from his belt in a speedy draw, the mouth of the barrel directed unwaveringly at Lance.

Lance's finger quivered on the trigger. He came within an ace of firing at the youngster in blue, then the realisation that he could not fire on one wearing the uniform of the United States Army any more than he could fire on a Sioux welled up in him.

It was a deadlock. The officer stood his ground, legs slightly apart, levelling his Colt at the man in the saddle who sat covering the young blue-coat with equal steadiness.

'Better put your gun up, Costigan,' said Lieutenant Soames.

'Yes, you'd better do that,' said Major Aitchison coldly from the background. He, too, was making a move for the revolver at his belt. As he finished the sentence, Aitchison jerked his head towards Lance in a signal to someone standing behind the man on the gelding and out of his range of vision.

Lance whirled about in the saddle, but a number of blue-coats who had been standing around at his back were already in action, swooping up on him.

Several strong hands clutched at Costigan's legs as the soldiers converged upon him. He half-slithered out of the saddle under their furious tugging. He tried to bring his Colt down, pistol-whip fashion, upon the head of a burly corporal who was lunging up at him with beefy fists, but someone grabbed his arm as it came down and yanked hard.

The Colt went falling from his grip as he fought to regain his balance in the saddle. Whoever had hold of his arm yanked harder and he went sprawling from his saddle into the knot of tough blue-coats, falling heavily to the snow-crusted ground.

He was breathless and furious as he came up from the ground, an all-consuming fury gripping him. He was only aware of a mass of blue-uniformed humanity surrounding him with flourishing fists. He saw a face under a peaked cavalry cap and smote at it with all the strength he could muster.

The blow connected with a meaty *thwack* and the owner of the face went teetering back with a squawk.

The mass of blue bodies and silver buttons closed in on Lance and fists came from all sides pummelling and punching. He tried to fight back and battle his way clear, but hadn't a chance against such odds. He didn't know whether he was fighting half-a-dozen or a dozen lusty troopers, but it seemed to him as though he was tackling the whole troop. He was breathless and fist-punished, a man drowning in a blue sea sprouting slamming fists, but he tried to lash out and claw at hostile bodies for what seemed to be an eternity.

He was blinded by blood, seeping from a cut one of the soldiers' blows had opened in his forehead and every last atom of air had been pounded from his lungs. He managed to locate the burly corporal and hand him a satisfyingly hefty blow in the midriff just before the whole world blacked out around him.

★ ★ ★

Costigan came to with a sensation akin to what he imagined a man would feel if a herd of crazy steers was stampeding over his head. He shook his head to get the world in focus and found he was sprawling among some trees close to the side of the creek.

Painfully, he pulled himself into a sitting position, looked down at his waist and found his gun-gear was missing.

'Ain't no good lookin' for your shootin' iron,' drawled a voice at his back. Lance turned about stiffly to see a youthful cavalryman squatting on a hummock, his back against a tree and his carbine levelled at him.

Costigan grunted.

'Looks like I'm a prisoner, all right.' He rubbed his aching head ruefully. 'How many of them blue-bellies attacked me?' he queried.

''Bout five,' replied the young soldier. He dropped his voice to a confidential whisper: 'Say, thanks for hitting Corporal Duffy so mighty hard — that guy's one of the worst non-coms in the troop!'

Lance quirked his blood-crusted lips into the best smile he could manage under the circumstances.

'Don't mention it, son. It was a pleasure. But they do say one good turn deserves another. Couldn't you kinda look the other way for a little while?'

'Not me,' the youngster retorted, canting his carbine into a more businesslike position. 'I'm detailed to keep watch on you an' that's what I aim to do — not that I have anythin' personal agin you.'

'Sure,' grunted Lance. 'I'm afraid your bull-headed major has plenty personal against me, though. He's content to have me packed back to Fort Yates and thrown in a guardhouse cell so the bad white *hombres* who're at the back of all this gun-smugglin' trouble get clear away. I guess that's what's known as the military mind — everythin' must be done accordin' to the book!'

The youthful trooper nodded in agreement.

'Yeah, that's Major Aitchison's style, for sure, an' he'd have my hide if I dared to turn my back an' let you run for it!'

Lance did not reply. He leaned against the bole of a tree and gazed at the activity down near the creek. Officers and soldiers were herding their Sioux prisoners into bundles while other blue-coats were busily disassembling the badly punished Gatling. Pretty soon, they'd be pushing off for the fort, he reflected, and he'd be among the prisoners. They would throw him into the stout log prison at Fort Yates while the sluggish military machinery turned out a charge of wilful damage to Government property against him — and those black-coated ones and Inskip ran for the clear!

He became aware of the sound of chomping jaws, turned his head slightly towards the direction of the sound and saw his gelding, still saddled, tethered only a few feet away in the grove.

If he could only sneak over to the still-saddled horse and get out of this spot — !

'Ain't no use a-watchin' that cayuse,' drawled the young trooper, as though he had been reading the half-breed's thoughts. 'If you made a move to jump aboard him, I'd have to shoot, an' I'd hate to have to do that to you — you bein' the feller that gave my ole enemy Corporal Duffy such an almighty swipe in the guts, an' all.'

Lance Costigan gave a disgruntled snort.

'Some day, you'll grow up to be a general, kid — you're a plumb vigilant soldier!'

From among the soldiers at the creek-side, one bearing the chevrons of a sergeant detached himself and walked slowly towards the grove of trees where Lance was kept under vigilance. The half-breed recognised the grizzled features of old Zeb Dockery.

Dockery entered the trees and jerked a nod of dismissal to the young blue-coat with the carbine.

'Okay, Smithers, you can dismiss — I'll watch him!'

The youth directed a wide-eyed stare at the old non-com who carried no weapon save the army model Colt holstered at his belt.

'Ain't you goin' to cover him, Sarge? The major said he's a dangerous galoot!'

'Never mind what the major said!' snapped old Zeb. 'This boy an' me have never been on gun-pointin' terms yet, an' I hope we never are!'

The youth dismissed a little non-plussed.

'A fine kettle of fish you mixed for

yourself!' observed Sergeant Dockery, seating himself on a dry tuft in the lee of a tree and facing Costigan. 'The major's hoppin' mad. Claims he's gonna throw the book at you for doin' what you did to that Gatlin'. He's been hollerin' that he won't stop short of havin' you clapped into the State Prison!'

'I had to do it, Zeb,' Costigan answered. 'I couldn't see the Indians in that village mown down like that!'

'Sure,' agreed Dockery. 'But orders are orders, son, an' a soldier has to obey 'em. The boys who were firin' the Gatlin' had to do as the major ordered.'

Lance pulled a wry face.

'The trouble with the fix I'm in right now, Zeb, is that the bad whites who are at the back of this trouble have a chance to get plumb clear while Aitchison goes through with his stupid military discipline.'

'Sure is gallin'.' the veteran agreed. 'But short of smackin' me over the jaw, you don't stand a chance of gettin' away!' There was a twinkle in the old-timer's eyes as he spoke — as though inviting the half-breed to try striking him.

'You don't think I'd ever hit you, Zeb?'

'Well, in the ordinary way, I'd say no, but bearin' in mind that you once told me that General Miles himself figured there was someone big at the back of the gun-runnin' I'd say it was your duty to go after them. Now, knowin' you to be the son of my old friend Malachy Costigan, I'd say you were made of the stuff that puts duty before personal feelin' an' you might very well hit an' old friend in a fix like the one you're in now. Then, again, if the big boys behind the gun-runnin' get plumb away because of the stupidity of our brass-necked major, we blue-bellies at Fort Yates will look plumb stupid when General Miles comes along wantin' to know why!'

Lance gathered himself up on his haunches, cast a quick glance at the preoccupied soldiers down near the creek and another at the gelding, cropping grass a few yards from him in the middle of the grove.

Zeb Dockery was only a matter of inches from him, sitting against the bole of the tree, his grizzled jaw held invitingly out and his faded eyes twinkling.

'You old fox!' grinned Lance. Then, he snaked his fist out in a quick arc to land a light blow on Zeb Dockery's bristly jaw.

The old soldier gave an exaggerated grunt and slumped against the tree with his eyes closed. Lance crouched close to the snow-whitened ground, unbuckled Dockery's gun-gear, put it around his own waist and began to edge slowly between the trees, moving towards the picketed gelding, Indian-fashion.

'I'll buy you a big drink for this, you old renegade,' he murmured to the old soldier before cat-footing out of earshot.

'You'll have to,' replied the supposedly unconscious old sergeant. 'I'll likely be busted down to trooper again for allowin' my prisoner to escape, an' I won't have enough money to buy my own drinks!'

Costigan moved deeper into the grove of trees, flattening himself close to the ground. When he reached his horse, he found that someone had fastened the rein around a tree-limb close enough to the ground for him to unfasten the hitch without standing. Bent double, he held the rein and 'injuned' his way through the snow-garlanded brush. Cautious backward glances revealed that the preparations for the troop to take their prisoners back to the fort were still going ahead down by the creek and he had not yet been missed from the isolated grove.

Steadily and patiently, he made his way through the stand of trees and down a slight declivity. Down here, he could not be seen by the main body of cavalry-men and he had a clear run from the Spring River reservation.

He mounted up quickly and touched spurs to hide.

10

Questions ran through Lance Costigan's head as he came out of the Spring River reservation at a smart lope.

What had happened to the three men who had hazed out of Lost Valley when Zeb Dockery's patrol arrived? Where were they now?'

Almost instinctively, his thoughts turned to Black Boulder. The two men from the Bismarck coach had been in the town on the previous night, he knew, would they head back there? Presumably, they had some kind of headquarters at Black Boulder, probably one of the three hotels. The chances of their heading back there and collecting their belongings to hightail from the vicinity were strong, so the half-breed turned the gelding's head in the direction of the prairie township.

He studied the sky, laden with the

promise of more snow. It was about five in the afternoon, he figured. From where he now was, an hour and a little more of riding would bring him to Black Boulder.

Relentlessly, he spurred the gelding onward. There was a pulsing hatred of the renegade white gun-smugglers pounding at his consciousness now. It had always been there, but now it was intensified by the action at Spring River. He saw those men — particularly the two in city clothing — as being responsible in their way for the deaths of Big Tree and White Buffalo as well as for the needless gunning of White Buffalo's camp. True, Shaintuck and the double-dealing Indian agent, Joe Folinsbee were dead, but the killer of Big Tree, Inskip, and the two black-clad ones who he knew to be the men behind the gun-running, were still at large.

He recalled the words the gunman, Quince, had shouted to him as he winged him in Lost Valley.

'*I'll get you one day, Costigan!*'

He only hoped the day he faced Luke Quince, the gunnie with the big reputation that had been built in the trigger-free days on the South-Western desert ranges, would be that self-same day!

Over the snow-glared plains, he rode like a man possessed. A wild, hatless figure, with his still-wet clothing clinging to his body, riding like an angel of retribution who packed a Colt .45.

★   ★   ★

'An hour,' said the man who now called himself Jethro Clute. 'A whole hour before the coach leaves!'

Mr Clute was not the happiest of men in the North-Western United States at the moment. He knew his double-dealing treachery was close to finding him out and his grandiose plans to make money out of the white man's red brothers had already crumbled somewhat.

It was one thing to sit in his law office in Bismarck and speculate on the dollars his agents in the Indian country were making on his behalf and quite another to sit in a dingy room in a prairie settlement hotel, knowing that the law or the army might show up before he could leave on the evening coach for Bismarck.

Clute had sound cause to feel jittery. His catspaws in the Indian reservation country had proved themselves hopeless bunglers. Their sideline of whiskey production had, in Clute's opinion, led to the failure of the gun-running activities. Shaintuck was dead, Moate may well be dead also, by this time, but young Inskip was alive, bullet-creased — and very jittery.

Inskip was slumped on a chair in the room, looking extremely dejected. The main reason for his dejection was the fact that he was without a gun, a condition which, to a youthful hothead of his calibre, was something akin to being without his clothing.

Luke Quince stood by the window, gazing down into the street. There was much of the old gun-slinging Quince about him now that many of the men who had known him in the old Arizona days would have recognised.

The black, square-cut coat was open, revealing the low-slung Colt around which Quince's long and bony fingers played restlessly. His flat, killer's eyes regarded the street intently, the thin lips were set in a grim line under his blade of a nose.

There was a thrill of impending action running through the gunfighter. He had been in this position of uncertain waiting, expecting to be confronted by officers of the law at every moment, many times in his life. They had only won out against him once and he wound up in the Arizona Territorial Prison. But there had been other times when the gun-crazy Quince came out of the gun-smoke victorious, to hit the owlhoot trail for other regions of the frontier.

He was one of the old bullet-breed and this tense waiting, this almost animal-like sensing of gun-prodding action in the offing, was life's blood to him.

Not so Jethro Clute. He was yellow right through, all he wanted at that moment was to climb aboard the evening coach and leave the plains country with a whole skin.

Inskip, gunless and with the threat of a murder charge for the killing of Big Tree hanging over him, was rendered the same yellow hue as the bearded, gun-running lawyer from Bismarck. He sprawled in the chair fidgeting nervously with his fingers.

Casting a backward glance at his two companions, Quince assessed their value if gun-trouble should come blasting around them.

It added up to a round nil.

Returning his gaze to the street below the window, Quince quirked his lips into a cold smile that went unseen by Clute and Inskip.

If the Army or the law came in smoking, he told himself, the first concern of Luke Quince would be to ensure a safe passage for Luke Quince! That had been the lesson he had learned in the man-proving crucible of the old days on the border-ranges. He had learned that maxim the hard way and it had kept him alive while a lot of the bullet-pushers of his younger days had found themselves boot-hill graves.

In Quince's book, a man stood alone when he stood with a bucking gun. If trouble busted loose — and he sensed that it was about to — he would scarcely spare a thought for the two weaklings at his back.

Down in the street of Black Boulder, he could see an enactment of languid activity as the dark shadows of evening sifted down over the straggle of clapboard and log buildings. One or two big-hatted cow-wranglers from the cattle-ranges picked their high-heeled way among the mud-puddles left by the snow or rode along the street on their rangy broncs. Here and there, the blue uniforms of off-duty soldiers from Fort Yates went into or came out of one of the saloons; a mule team hauling a creaky wagon went sloshing through the mud, its oldster of a driver bellowing hoarsely at the animals; an Indian woman with her baby slung on her back went shuffling along the far plank-walk — and a bedraggled rider, tall in the saddle, came into view, sitting his gelding at a steady walk.

Luke Quince's eyes widened.

'Costigan!' he half-whispered. 'Out on the street!'

Clute and Inskip moved as though each had received a simultaneous electric shock. Both jumped to their feet and joined the lean, gun-packer at the window. Through the grubby lace curtains, they watched the tall half-breed.

'Looks like he's sore as blazes,' murmured Quince slowly. 'Wonder where his pals the soldiers are.'

'He's on his own,' squeaked the

jittery Inskip. 'I guess he's lookin' for us. By grab, if I had a gun, I could plug him from here!'

'Sure,' agreed Clute, as edgy as Inskip. 'We could get him from here without any trouble at all!'

'Use your heads — both of you!' rapped Quince, coldly. 'We don't want to start no gunplay from a rat-trap like this. I like to have space around me before I start throwin' slugs. Besides, he's talkin' to the marshal now.'

Down on the street, Lance Costigan had pulled his mount to a halt and was in conversation with Marshal Otto Gantz who was leaning his big body against the hitch-rack outside his office.

'Right across from us,' grumbled Inskip. 'We could plug him easy!'

Luke Quince turned with the light, cat-footed about-turn common to his kind.

'An' I say that'd be a fool move!' he grated. 'Like I told you, Inskip — use your head. I don't want to hear no ideas from a guy that can't even make good at an easy chore like back-shootin' a galoot. If there's any gun-throwin' to be thought out, leave it to me!'

'Wonder what Costigan an' the marshal are talkin' about,' said Clute, peering anxiously through the pane.

'Probably fixin' to come over here lookin' for us,' opined Inskip. 'It's easy for you guys to stand there an' talk. You only got the gun-runnin' charges to worry about, but they'll want to stretch my neck for killin' that Injun, Big Tree. Things ain't what they was any more. You can't get away with killin' an Injun just because he's an Injun! An' I ain't got a gun to defend myself with, either!'

Luke Quince bestowed another cold glance upon the young gunslinger, causing him to lapse into silence. All three gazed down at the hatless, fist-punished half-breed on the gelding where he sat holding conversation with the peace-officer of Black Boulder.

Marshal Otto Gantz had hailed Lance as the tall, copper-skinned rider came into the evening-shrouded town.

The astute marshal did not fail to notice the signs of recent rough usage about Costigan's face and the fact that his clothes had lately been wet. He wondered, too, why Costigan wore an army belt and revolver in place of his usual cowhand's gun-gear.

'Hi, Lance!' called Gantz. 'You look plumb peaked an' kinda sore! Fact is, you look mighty like a man on the prod.'

'I'm on the prod, all right, Otto. Lookin' for the city galoots that were in town earlier, the guys in black suits who came in on the evenin' coach last night; you seen them around?'

The marshal eyed the half-breed with a cool, calculating glance. He looked a slow-thinking and slow-moving man this big, square-headed lawman, but his looks belied his temperament. He went through life with both eyes wide open and his shrewd mind turning over like a well-oiled machine — which was why he had survived his many years of star-packing.

'You lookin' for them city galoots on Army business, Lance?' he inquired with the same casual air he might have employed in making idle conversation about the weather.

'Army business an' personal business. There's a polecat with them that tried to bushwhack me once an' the same feller is the one that killed Big Tree when he got the Indian drunk an' they fell out over a gun-runnin' deal. I figured they'd be here at one of the hotels.'

'You figured right, son,' the lawman answered. 'They're at the Palace, all three of them. Saw them come in earlier an' go into the Palace. That's where they stayed after arrivin' last night.'

'The hell it was!' swore Costigan, thinking that he had slept at the Dakota Palace himself the previous night and had been under the same roof as the men behind the gun-running racket without knowing it.

'An old-timer told me he figured the

thin one was Luke Quince, the gunfighter, Lance. If he is Quince, you might need plenty of help; that guy has a big reputation.'

'I'll handle it alone, thanks. I figure I can face up to Luke Quince — men with big reputations have been known to get well ventilated before today,' the half-breed replied.

'Suit yourself,' answered the marshal. 'I'll keep my eyes open an' if you look like you need any help, I'll come with my gun smokin'!'

'Much obliged,' Costigan replied and he angled his horse off across the street towards the Dakota Palace.

Neither he nor the marshal had any idea that the three men Costigan was seeking watched them from the window of their room at the hotel.

Up in the room, both Clute and Inskip were in a jittery condition.

'He's comin' over here,' yipped the bearded lawyer, jumping back a pace from the window.

'He ain't gettin' me!' squawked

Inskip, a high edge to his voice. He was standing close to Jethro Clute and he made a sudden, swift grab for the Colt the crooked lawyer wore at his belt. Before either Clute or Quince realised what was happening Inskip had whipped the gun clear of leather. He sped to the window, parted the curtains, and shattered a hole in the glass with the barrel of the weapon.

Down on the gloomy street, Lance was in the act of hitching his horse outside the hotel. The sound of breaking glass was a warning to him. At the same time, from behind him, Otto Gantz's voice called:

'Look out, Lance! The window!'

Costigan whirled down into a gun-slinger's crouch, his right hand blurring for the weapon he had 'borrowed' from Zeb Dockery. At the same instant, Inskip fired. The spurt of flame slashed out of the hole the youngster had made in the window. Lance, gun in hand, slewed his body to one side as the slug tore a splinter from the hitch-rack.

The shot was hopelessly wide because Quince, with the sudden realisation of what Inskip was about to do, grabbed him in an attempt to prevent him shooting.

But the lean gunslinger was a split second too late. He hoisted Inskip away from the window, grabbing his gun-arm with talon-like fingers. Quince applied the pressure of a steel vice and the Colt dropped from the other's hand.

'You damn fool,' snarled Quince, his face twisted into a mask of rage. 'You've given away our position — we're holed up in here now! That blasted half-breed an' the marshal can fire on us all they want now, if we dare to show our faces at the window!'

He hit Inskip a savage blow across the jaw, sending him reeling across the bed. Jethro Clute, anticipating a holocaust of hot lead to be loosed upon the hotel room via the window, was flattened wide-eyed against a far wall.

Down on the darkening street, Lance, expecting more shooting from the window, had angled close to the structure of the hotel, gun at the ready.

On the other side of the mud-puddled street, Marshal Gantz, his big Peacemaker Colt in his beefy hand, had sought the shelter of the law-office door, ready to return any fire from the Dakota Palace. The street of Black Boulder had cleared at the first shot, the citizenry having taken to any available cover in great haste.

There was no further shooting from the hotel window.

Tension mounted high as scared faces peered around doorways and out of windows along the town's single street.

'You guys up there!' bawled Costigan. 'You better give yourselves up before we come in blastin'!'

Luke Quince edged close to the window and took a quick look into the deepening shadows of the street. He could see Costigan, standing quite close to the building and the big figure of Gantz on the opposite plank-walk. He ducked back when he saw the marshal make a quick movement with his gun.

Quince eyed the gloomy room. Jethro Clute was still flattened against the far wall and Inskip was seated on the bed, holding his jaw ruefully.

'There must be a back way out of here,' the gunman said icily. 'If we can get out that way, we might stand a chance of grabbin' horses an' high-tailin'. I seem to remember a livery-stable on this side of the street. Once we get into the back alleys, we can make our way there an' grab a couple of cayuses.' At the back of his mind ran his old maxim that a man stood alone in any gun-trouble and once he was clear of the rat-trap, that was exactly what he'd be doing.

'How do we know the back ain't watched as well as the front?' asked Inskip, from the bed. 'That marshal has deputies, y'know!'

'We don't know,' retorted the gun-fighter. 'But it's dark enough for us to take the chance.' His thin lips suddenly curled back into a hard smile and he added: 'Anyway, you don't have to worry none, Inskip — you won't be comin' along!'

Inskip was on his feet at once.

'What d'you mean?' he wanted to know.

Luke Quince moved towards him rapidly. At the same time, his gun-hand flashed downwards and it streaked up with a fistful of Colt revolver covering the youngster.

'I mean what I say, Inskip — you ain't comin' along,' he repeated. His voice was completely toneless.

From outside, the voice of Costigan came echoing once more:

'You guys better come down here empty handed — you have nothin' to gain but bullets!'

Clute watched the gunman covering Inskip, wondering what was going on behind that cold, killer's face.

'What you aimin' to do?' he asked. The precise lawyer-talk he employed in Bismarck had now slipped entirely, as had his air of being the big man pulling the strings. The dominant character now was Luke Quince while Clute had been reduced to very small fry.

'Pick up that gun, Jethro, an' you'll find out,' Quince said. As he finished speaking, he made a lunge for the scared Inskip, grabbed him by the arm and whirled him about, forcing the captive arm up his back, causing a squeak of pain to come from the young gunnie's lips. 'Inskip's been a bungler all along, Jethro,' he said. 'He got mixed up with Shaintuck's hobby of booze-peddlin', he killed an Injun because of it, he couldn't even make a good job of bushwhackin' a guy on his own admission an' now he ain't even got a gun to hold off those guys on the street — after givin' our position away by that fool move! He's goin' out on the street — I'm throwin' him to the dogs!'

'No!' protested Inskip. '*You can't do it*!'

'Can't I?' leered Quince. 'You're no use around here Inskip. You're on your way out, to give me — and Clute — a chance to run for it.'

He almost omitted to add that 'and Clute'.

Savagely he twisted Inskip's arm with his free hand and rammed the Colt into the small of his back with the other. He propelled the younger man towards the door, with Jethro Clute trailing in his wake.

'Open the door, Jethro,' ordered the gunman.

Clute obeyed and Quince led the way, shoving the protesting Inskip before him, along a gloomy corridor and down the stairs which gave onto the wide bar-room of the Dakota Palace. The scrubby, bearded barkeep and one or two customers stood around the bar, apprehensive of trouble about to burst loose on the street.

'Keep 'em covered, Jethro,' snapped Quince, as he shoved Inskip down the stairway. 'Don't any of you galoots make a move for your hardware!'

The barkeep and his patrons stood stock-still, backing up against the bar and keeping their hands in full view.

The rumour that the tall, lean, black-garbed man was Luke Quince, the Arizona gunslinger, had circulated around Black Boulder and no one in the bar-room wanted to tangle with one with his bullet-throwing reputation.

They stood mutely watching the tall gunman shove his captive towards the batwing doors. Arrived there, Quince stopped some little distance from the doors, crouching low. Then he shoved Inskip with all his might to send the youngster spinning through the batwings.

'Let 'em gun you!' he snarled after the staggering youngster as he went headlong through the pivoting doors. Then he turned on his heel and went haring along the bar-room, heading for the back of the hotel.

'C'mon!' he yelled at Clute. The Bismarck lawyer went panting at his heels like a scared puppy.

Lance Costigan was on the gallery of the Dakota Palace, about to enter the hotel, when the stumbling form of

Inskip came through the batwings.

Marshal Gantz was halfway across the street, walking cautiously with his Peacemaker at the ready.

It was dark on the gallery and the half-breed was given a glimpse of the stumbling man's face as he staggered through a shaft of yellow light thrown from one of the windows of the saloon-cum-hotel. He recognised the features as being those of the man he thought of as Yellow Slicker, the killer of White Buffalo's son and the man who had tried to back-shoot him in the outcrop of the badlands.

Costigan threw the muzzle of his gun up and was about to fire when Marshal Gantz yelled, urgently:

'He ain't got a gun, Lance!'

Costigan's trigger-finger stilled when it was just about to send a slug slamming into Inskip. He jerked out his free hand and plucked at Inskip's shirt, pulling the youngster towards him and ramming the Colt into his midriff.

'Don't shoot!' panted Inskip, his

208

body quivering from top to toe. 'The others are headin' out back — makin' for the livery-stable!'

'What's the idea — flingin' you out this way?' asked Lance, prodding Inskip with his gun. 'Are they riggin' some kind of gun-trap?'

'It's no gun-trap,' blurted Inskip. 'They ditched me 'cause they figured I'm an encumbrance, damn 'em. They reckoned you'd gun me down an' give them a chance to hightail.'

'You prepared to testify against those guys?' asked Lance, his dark eyes flashing.

'I'll testify, all right,' grated the other. 'If I'm gettin' mine, I'll testify enough to make sure those two snakes get theirs. Maybe I'll get leniency for turnin' State's evidence, huh?' he added, hopefully.

'I wouldn't count on that,' Costigan snorted sourly. He yanked the young gun-runner over towards the steps of the gallery and shoved him down them towards where the marshal stood.

'He's your prisoner, Otto,' the half-breed called. 'You can put two charges against him by way of a start. The murder of Big Tree an' attempted murder in which I nearly played the part of the corpse.'

Gantz grabbed Inskip as he came tumbling down the steps.

'Looks like this is your night for gettin' pushed around, mister,' he remarked. Gantz saw the shadowy figure of Costigan on the hotel gallery making for the batwings, gun held tense.

'If you're goin' in there — watch out!' the peace-officer cautioned.

'I'm watchin',' came the terse reply from the half-breed. Then he kicked the batwings open and went in.

11

All was quiet inside the bar-room of the Dakota Palace.

At the bar stood the patrons and the scrubby, bearded barkeep, their heads swivelled about to face the batwings through which Costigan came at a gunfighter's crouch.

'The galoots who threw that feller out on to the street — where are they?' he rapped.

The barkeep jerked his head in the direction of a small door at the furthermost end of the room.

'Through there,' he directed. 'Watch your step, they both have guns!'

Lance made for the door, treading cautiously, half-expecting a roar of gunfire to greet him as he flung it open. The room was a kitchen, empty save for a dazed Chinese cook sitting among the shambles of cooking gear scattered on the floor. A small frame door across the kitchen swung open against the night.

'What happened, Charlie?' asked Lance of the rueful featured Chinese.

'Two fellers come runnin' through, wavin' guns,' twittered the oriental from his seat on the wooden floor. 'Come pushin' into Charlie's kitchen in big hully. Charlie in middle of cookin' pie an' fellers push him one side an' go runnin' out of door into alley — all good glub go bang on floor, Charlie, too!'

Costigan made for the smaller door and cursed himself for being a stupid fool, maybe the punishment he'd taken from those ham-fisted blue-bellies had knocked him into idiocy. Inskip had said the men he sought would make for the livery-stable to get possession of horses; he should have made for the stable by way of the street and waylaid them there instead of trying this fool play of chasing them through the hotel. However, he would have to go through with this method of pursuit now he had embarked upon it.

The alley was wide, running at the rear of all the buildings on that side of the street of Black Boulder. It was trash-scattered, and its night-shrouded length was illuminated only by the occasional yellow square of a back window.

Stepping out of the rear door of the hotel kitchen, Costigan caught a sudden running movement silhouetted against one such lighted window. He could hear the thumping of more than one pair of feet running about thirty yards away.

He triggered a wild shot into the darkness, firing in the direction of the sound. The running feet, stumbling over scattered litter, echoed after the slamming of the six-gun died and Lance set off running in pursuit.

From up ahead, the slash of gunfire rent the blackness and a bullet whined past him, a hasty shot, fired by a running man. Still running, Lance doubled his body into a low crouch.

Stumbling over the unseen cans and discarded bottles that littered the ground, he fired again. Up ahead was an intersection of the alley where the tall structure of the livery-stable stood out to one side. There was a dim flash of light from a window somewhere, illuminating the smaller lane crossing the wide alley. Against it, he saw two figures silhouetted for a brief instant. Without slackening the pace of his running, he fired and one of the figures sagged with a hoarse yelp.

'Quince, I'm hit in the leg!'

Costigan saw the second silhouette, tall and ghost-like against the feeble glow of light, hoist the second one into the lee of a clapboard wall. Then, a glittering gun was flourished in the wash of light and a red tongue of flame came slashing in his direction, followed a split-second afterwards by a bellowing bark made louder by the confined space.

Costigan tried to duck to the ground, but the agony of a biting bullet tore hotly at his left shoulder.

With a loud, involuntary yell, he stumbled and hit the foul floor of the alleyway with all the world whirling about him. Through a red haze of pain, he was dimly aware of a triumphant voice yelling:

'I hit him!' Then came the sound of running feet once more and a long silence in which he was aware only of his wounded shoulder, the pounding of his heart and his heavy, groan-interspersed breathing.

The sound of horses' hoofs reached him through the curtain of pain. Hoofs pounding away into the distance.

Mechanically, he pulled his body up from the ground, spitting the dirt of the alley from his mouth.

'Damn them!' he thought. 'They're gettin' clear away!'

He staggered up on unsteady legs and leaned heavily against a rough wall, panting like a half-drowned dog. The urgency of the need to pursue the gun-runners pounded madly at his consciousness. He staggered onward in the direction of the livery-stable, crimson fury gnawing at him.

At the intersection of the alley and the smaller lane, there was an ominous silence and the high door of the livery stable yawned blackly. Costigan dragged himself through it, aware of the silence broken only by the restless stirring of the horses tethered in the stalls lining either side of the stable. The gloomy building held the typical musk of such a place, compounded of the odours of horse-droppings, oats and saddle-leather.

In entering the door, Lance stumbled over a still form, lying prone in the hoof-pounded dirt. He squatted beside the sprawled figure, thinking at first that the man was dead.

Dimly, he realised the man on the ground was Ed Culver, the owner of the stable. He was still breathing and began to groan as Lance shook him.

'Ed, what happened? Did they plug you?' he husked.

'No,' grunted the liveryman. 'Took a couple of my horses an' one of 'em socked me over the head with his gun as they lit out!'

'Took the out-trail, eh, Ed — the badlands trail?'

'I guess so, they'd hardly ride through town if they were bein' chased. Who are they, anyway? What in tarnation's all the ruckus about?'

'I've no time to explain now, Ed. You got a really fast horse in here?'

'Try the piebald in the first stall, he's plenty fast,' answered Culver, rising unsteadily to his feet. 'Wait until I strike a match an' get the lantern lit, I'll get you a saddle an' bridle.'

'Don't worry about any saddle,' grunted Lance, already weaving an unsteady course for the stall housing the piebald. 'I'll make do with just a bridle an' bit.'

Culver produced a match and lighted a storm lantern, crossed to a selection of trappings hanging from one of the walls and produced a bridle and bit. He handed them to the half-breed, viewing him critically in the yellow glow of the lamp.

'You don't look any too good, Lance,' he observed. 'You sure you're fit to ride out after those galoots?'

'I have a slug in my shoulder, but I'm ridin' after that pair if it's the last thing I ever do,' Costigan informed the livery-stable owner.

'It'll take Injun ridin' skill to keep forkin' that critter without a saddle,' Culver said, with a nod towards the piebald.

'I'm half Sioux, ain't I?' replied the other, swinging stiffly up to the animal's back.

'Which means you have a plumb good chance of overtakin' 'em,' Culver said, philosophically. 'They took out of here on them stolen cayuses so damn fast they didn't even pause to saddle 'em!'

Lance took cartridges from the loops in the black military belt at his waist and slipped them into the empty chambers of his revolver.

'Run along the street, Ed, an' tell Marshal Gantz I've taken off after those galoots on the badlands trail. He can come trailin' with a posse if things go badly with me,' he instructed Culver. Then he touched his spurs to the piebald and went pounding out of the stable door.

Culver's stable stood at a point where the single street of Black Boulder straggled away to become the back-trail leading out in the direction of the badlands. Costigan wheeled the saddle-less piebald into the street at a speedy lick, holding his legs tightly against the animal's ribs, rodeo-rider fashion. The slug in his shoulder ached furiously and he felt as though a wild bronco was kicking madly at the base of his skull.

Doggedly, he spurred the pony onward. The lights of the town slipped behind him and the trail snaked through the gloom of the open plains, across which the winter wind, laden with the threat of snow, whipped in chilly gusts.

Up ahead, lurking in the distant darkness, were the Dakota badlands, through which the trail snaked into Wyoming.

'Hell with the fires out' men called the wild tangle of peaks and meandering canyons and Lance knew well that, once the men he was trailing reached the labyrinthine ways of the badlands, his chances of locating them would be extremely thin.

Head bent low, he spurred the piebald through the blackness, splitting the wind, his long hair streaming behind him. He had no knowledge of how long he had been riding before he heard the double tattoo of two running horses drumming ahead of him. Teeth clenched against the throb of the pain of his wounded shoulder, he rowelled the hide of the pony savagely.

Up ahead, Quince and Clute were riding their saddleless mounts with difficulty. Clute was slumped on the back of his mount, holding his side, into which Costigan's slug had ripped during the chase in the alleyway. His breath was sounding in painful, soughing gasps and he was having trouble in keeping astride the stolen mount.

Riding beside him, Luke Quince was showing signs of impatience. Hitting the owl-hoot trail with a wounded partner was not for him. He was the lone lobo type when the going was at its toughest. His way in a spot like this was to stand with a lone gun and look out for his own interests.

'C'mon, Jethro. Get some more life out of that cayuse!' he growled without a spark of sympathy for the injured man. Clute was sighing painfully in the darkness beside the gunman.

'Take it easy, Luke. This damn slug is givin' me hell. Can't we take a rest for a while?'

'If you rest, you're on your own,' Quince retorted sharply. 'Now, get a spurt out of that cayuse!'

Clute, half-slithering from the bare back of the horse, tried to kick it into quicker action with his spurless heels. The effort made him gasp with pain and claw at his injured side.

Quince cast him a contemptuous glance that was lost in the darkness. They pounded onward through the night, two shadowy riders on the wind-scythed trail.

Luke Quince was thinking his own private thoughts, mostly concerned with how much of an encumbrance the gun-running Bismarck lawyer was going to be in getting clear of this territory.

The gunslinger stiffened on his horse's back as a distant sound assailed his ears. The sound of an approaching horse, drumming louder and nearer behind them.

'Hit that cayuse into a faster run,' he snarled to his companion. 'There's someone on our tail!'

'A posse!' exclaimed Clute. In the darkness, his face was contorted with pain as he kicked at his horse and tried to pull himself into a safer position on the animal's back. Quince was listening to the approaching hoof-beats with the practised ear of one who had taken the back-trail out of many towns on many occasions. He grabbed his gun and cleared his holster with the lightning action of a slug-slinger.

'That ain't a posse,' he declared. 'Sounds like just one rider! C'mon, get the lead out of that critter's feet!'

Clute gasped in pain, trying to urge more speed out of the horse under him. He suddenly gave a panicky screech. Quince turned his head to see the ill-defined shape of the man who rode beside him slithering from the bare back of his mount.

'*Luke! Grab me — I'm slippin' off*!' mouthed Clute.

The gunman saw his companion go pitching from the back of his mount with a hoarse squeak which sounded above the ever increasing hoof-drum of the pursuing rider's horse. Quince snarled in the darkness and kicked more speed out of his horse.

Clute's voice came from down near

the ground, screeching like a frightened child's:

'Luke! Don't leave me!'

Quince turned his head and bawled into the wind: 'You have a gun, hold him off with it!' And he added to himself: 'So I stand a better chance of gettin' into the badlands.'

Costigan, drumming up close behind, heard the exchange above the pounding of hoofs and the rushing sigh of the prairie wind. Dimly, he could discern a madly ridden horse hightailing up-trail and a riderless one close behind it. It dawned on his benumbed brain that Clute must have fallen from his mount and would be lying somewhere on the trail. He had no notion of how near he was to the fallen man until Clute fired, sending a bullet scorching Lance's temple.

The half-breed's mount, scared by the sudden shot, reared high, almost throwing its rider from its back. Lance grabbed and drew the army Colt at his belt and fired in the direction of the muzzle-flash that betrayed the where-abouts of the man on the trail. He ducked low into the horse's mane as an answering flash came out of the darkness and another angry hornet of lead zoomed over his head.

This time, he marked Clute's tell-tale flame of powder-flash carefully and fired twice in its direction. An agonised gurgle issued out of the wind-whipped blackness and Lance fired twice in the direction of the sound.

No answering shot came.

Costigan sat his mount for a long instant.

There was only the sound of the wind scything the wide prairie in its restless gusts and the distance-thinned wail of a coyote in the nearby badlands. The sounds of the retreating fugitive had almost disappeared into the vault of the wide distance, but he could hear them drumming faintly.

He swung down from the pony, walked cautiously in the direction from which the shooting came, pistol levelled and trigger-finger tensed. Maybe the fellow was lying doggo, waiting for just such a move as this on Costigan's part to slam a slug into him.

Damn the fiery pain of the bullet in his shoulder and damn the wild bronco that was still kicking at the base of his brain!

He found the crumpled form of the man he had shot, a dark splotch spread-eagled on the trail. Kneeling on the hard-crusted snow, he put up his gun and fished with difficulty for his matches. The thick material of his quilted slicker had kept them dry through his exploits at the creek on Spring River reservation. He struck one and surveyed the death-twisted form of the man he had killed. A white death-mask of a face, fringed with fashionable whiskers, stared up at him. The corpse, in its black, city-cut clothing looked oddly out of place on this bleak Dakota plain.

Costigan located the horse the dead man had been riding, turned its head towards Black Boulder and hit it a hard spank across the rump. It hazed off towards the distant township and he knew it would follow its instinct until it arrived at Ed Culver's stable.

Wearily, with fingers of blazing agony tearing at his injured shoulder and the crazy bronco still kicking at his brain, he mounted the piebald once more and spurred it up the trail.

Somewhere up there, possibly lost by now in the twisting tangles of the notorious badlands, was the lean gun-hawk with the big reputation, Luke Quince.

He remembered how, when he lay on the rafter in the cabin at Lost Valley, he heard Quince voice the opinion that he would 'admire' to have him on the business-end of his shooting-iron and the echo of the lean slug-slinger's shout as he rode out of the valley sounded once more in his feverish brain:

'I'll get you one day, Costigan!'

To Costigan, facing Quince and gunning it out with him had taken on a towering importance, surmounting the business of running guns to the dance-crazed Sioux. Quince represented a type of humanity that belonged essentially to the bloody days of the wide-open frontier.

Clutching his mount tightly with his knees, hand on the butt of the revolver he had taken from old Zeb Dockery, mindful of the fact that the man he sought might be lurking somewhere beside the trail to gun him down, Lance Costigan rode for the badlands.

Half of his mind was sinking into delirium now. He was aware of the pounding throb in his left shoulder; he was aware of encroaching delirium, trying to steal his reason like a thief entering his head. He shook his head frequently to drive it away. Sometimes he spoke aloud to himself. His aching head was full of echoing nonsense, mingled ghost-dance chants and gunfire; bearded death-masks of gun-dealing lawyers and lean, blade-nosed features of bullet-throwing gunnies; Gatling fire and screaming squaws and children.

Luke Quince was resting his horse beside the trail where it snaked into the crazy maze of the badlands when he heard the approach of the pursuing rider.

He grabbed his Colt and cleared leather.

He had thought himself reasonably safe, having heard no sound of further pursuit since he had left his partner lying on the trail. Hightailing for the badlands, he had heard the exchange of gunfire in his wake and reasoned that either Clute or the pursuer was now dead with the survivor probably in bad enough shape to preclude his following up the trail. Now, the sound of an approaching horse was in his ears.

By grab, he did not want the company of whoever was riding after him! Clute, in his shot-up condition, was a hindrance and the other guy, whoever he was, was his natural enemy, a man on his tail in the name of what weak fools considered law and order.

Silently, Luke Quince climbed down

from his saddleless mount, caught a hank of its mane in his hand and led it up a gentle slope rising from the edge of the trail. The slope was shale, with crusty top of snow and the going was not easy for man and horse. Quince made all the haste he could. The loud-sounding thump of the running horse down-trail was now very close.

The gunman found scattered boulders tumbled in the snow-whitened shale. Pulling the horse by the mane, he forced it into a kneeling position behind one of these and crouched into the cover of the boulder, with naked gun at the ready.

Whoever was in pursuit had to pass below him now and he could gun them with ease, whether it was Clute or the lone rider who had exchanged shots with the man he had left on the trail.

The eerie silence of the badland peaks brooded about him and he felt that old tingle he had always known when his trigger-finger was itchy. He was in his old position once more; Luke

Quince looking out for no one but Luke Quince.

And the pounding hoofbeats drew nearer.

Costigan came along the gloomy trail, a man in a half-dream world, the jagged peaks of 'Hell with the fires out' brooding on all sides. His piebald mount suddenly threw back its head and snorted a brief whinny. From up the shaley, snow-crusted drift to his right, came the answering whinny of another animal, only a matter of yards away.

Lance's befuddled wits cleared as the last note of the nickering echoed away. Hidden Indian instincts seemed to come into play from somewhere deep in his being, overriding the pain of his shoulder and the half-delirium that gripped his mental faculties.

He flung himself from the back of the horse as a barking six-gun sounded from behind the rock, sending a slug whining past his ear and a flat echo clattering along the devious ways of the badlands.

He hit the ground with a thud that

sent a jarring pain through his injured shoulder, recovered his breath, dragged the army Colt from its holster and lay waiting. The Indian in him was dominating his action now. He lay completely still, watching the rock cluster from which the tell-tale whinny and the shot had issued.

Slowly, the silhouette of a man rose from behind the rock.

'Comin' to see if I'm dead,' thought Lance, clenching his teeth against the blaze of pain in his shoulder.

He waited until the figure had emerged fully from the cover of the rocks and he triggered a slug at him.

The man further up the drift of shale howled a yelp of pain and went dancing backwards on his heels. Lance cursed his position on the ground and his unsteady gun-hand as he saw his adversary scooting back into his cover.

Although it brought an almost unbearable agony to his injured shoulder, he rolled over to his left half-a-dozen times and began to crawl forward. From behind his cover of rock, Quince fired two wild shots at the spot where the half-breed's muzzle-flash had shown itself a minute before.

Costigan was close to the other's cover now, he gathered himself up into a crouching position and moved forward as quickly as was possible on the snow-covered shale. He was wheezing and panting involuntarily now and Quince, a newly-ploughed bullet-furrow over one ear, heard the sound. He whipped around, had a brief glimpse of a figure lunging forward towards him and near enough for him to distinguish the drawn, Indian-like features and the flashing black eyes.

The stumbling apparition bellowed out a half-crazed yell:

'Come on, Quince, gun it out! Defend your big reputation!'

Luke Quince fired a panicky shot, the bullet merely plucking at Lance's sleeve, then three white slashes of fire stabbed out from the half-breed's hand.

Luke Quince felt the shattering slam

of the slugs pounding into his frame. He tripped forward on his toes, walking two or three drunken paces, then he hit the snow-carpeted shale face first, slithering down the drift for several yards like a limp doll. Death, an old acquaintance who had stood close to his gun-arm many times in places such as Tombstone, Nogales and El Paso, gathered him into its arms at last.

12

Dawn broke with a leaden coldness and brought the first wind-slanted flakes of the long-threatened blizzard.

On the badlands trail between the barren tangle of peaks and Black Boulder, Marshal Otto Gantz and a group of Black Boulder citizens sat their horses, regarding the corpse of Jethro Clute, alias Jerry Cray, sprawling on the frozen ground.

'So that was the big brain behind the gun-runnin' racket,' he murmured. 'That Inskip guy I slapped into the cell back in Black Boulder sure squawked plenty about this galoot. A big-shot lawyer in Bismarck with a gun-runnin' racket out here!'

The posse from Black Boulder had been hastily raised by the marshal after Ed Culvert brought him the news that Luke Costigan had taken the badlands trail after the pair of gun-runners. Earlier, they had found the saddleless horse which Costigan had sent hazing in the townward direction and Culvert, riding with the group, identified it as one of the pair taken from his stable. Following the trail, they came upon the body of the bewhiskered Bismarck lawyer, proof that Costigan had paid out at least one of the fugitives.

Ed Culvert, sitting his horse, suddenly craned his neck to take in a fuller view of the trail ribboning through the slanting snow in the direction of the badlands.

'Hey, Otto, take a look along the trail!' he exclaimed. 'It's Costigan!'

The party from Black Boulder watched the snow-dusted trail in silence. Out of the badlands, they saw two saddleless horses approaching. On one, sat the slumped figure of the half-breed; on the second, which he led by a hank of its mane, was draped a corpse.

The men of the posse sat their

saddles in the increasing snow, waiting for the copper-skinned rider with the strained, trail-hollowed features and the limp left arm to draw closer to them. His hatless head was powdered with the fresh snow and his black eyes flashed with an unusual brightness.

'You can turn back, boys,' he called to the posse in a voice little more than a croak. 'This is Luke Quince — the gun-runners are all accounted for!'

Then, he flopped over the neck of his mount in a dead faint.

★   ★   ★

When he came round, Lance found himself lying on the bunk of one of the cells at the rear of Marshal Gantz's office. He gathered his scattered wits and found that the lawman and Sergeant Zeb Dockery were standing close to him. Someone had dressed the wound in his shoulder and he was strapped up in clean bandages.

''Bout time you woke up,' declared

the big marshal, with a grin. 'You slept for hours an' hours.' He ducked into the outer office and returned with a pot of hot coffee and a large cup.

'Get some of this inside you, Lance,' he ordered, 'then wait a few minutes while I rustle up some bacon an' beans for you.'

Costigan sat up on the bunk, taking the proffered coffee gratefully.

'I guess you been sent to arrest me for that game I played with the Gatlin', eh, Zeb?' he asked the cavalry non-com.

'Nope,' replied the veteran. 'I got back to the fort with the rest of the troop an' our prisoners an' rested up awhile. Then I heard about you fixin' those gun-runnin' galoots an' that you were here in town. I was free of duty, so I rode in to see you.'

'You didn't get busted down to trooper for allowin' your prisoner to get away?'

'I got the raw edge of Major Aitchison's tongue for about fifteen minutes,' admitted Zeb. 'The fact that you fixed those galoots has kind of exonerated you, son. The fact is, you won't get any kicks for that business with the Gatlin', either. Things have been happenin' all over the scenery an' Aitchison will be plumb eager to have the fact that he opened up with the Gatlin' forgotten!'

'What d'you mean, things have been happenin'?' queried Lance.

'Well, Lance, the ghost-dance troubles are over. They were pretty pitiful, but could have got really bad if those gun-runnin' galoots went the full distance with their repeater an' fire-water tradin'. They didn't, thanks to you. Anyway, Sittin' Bull's dead an' the army acted in a plumb stupid way down at Wounded Knee Creek — heads are goin' to roll for what they did, that's why Aitchison will want that Gatlin' incident forgotten!'

'Sittin' Bull dead?' echoed Lance. 'And what happened at Wounded Knee Creek?'

'The Government made an order for

Sittin' Bull to be arrested, since he was obviously the man behind the ghost-dance mania,' explained Dockery. 'A crowd of Indian police went to his camp on Grand River the other mornin' to take him. Sittin' Bull began to go quietly at first, then he got ornery an' Sergeant Red Tomahawk shot him dead. That loosed off a big fight, but the police an' troops that was with 'em settled the Sioux. Then the Sioux down at Wounded Knee got wind of the old Chief's death an' began to mass for trouble. Colonel Forsyth an' a bunch of cavalry surrounded the camp at Wounded Knee an' things looked quiet while the blue-coats began to disarm the redskins. Then a crazy medicine-man named Yellow Bird made the sign for fight an' the Sioux opened up on the soldiers.

'The soldiers had to begin shooting. It was a massacre, Lance. Women an' kids were killed an' the soldiers, raw rookies, most of 'em, were even killin' each other in their own crossfire. They stopped all signs of fight from the Sioux, but some heads will roll for the way the situation was handled. That's why the major will be glad to forget about his rash use of the Gatlin' at Spring River.'

Lance listened to the story of the quelling of the Sioux with pursed lips. The ghost-dance craze had been pitiful and might have remained harmless, but for the interference of gun-running whites. Now it had ended in the massacre of squaws and children at Wounded Knee Creek. That action was to go down in history as the last time United States troops clashed with the Sioux.

The Sioux were finished as fighting men. Lance realised that as he ate the meal Otto Gantz put into his hands. The proud warriors of the Hunkpapa Sioux, once ferocious hunters and soldiers of the plains would be only a memory from now on. Their death-knell had been the chatter of guns and the screams of the dying at Wounded Knee.

Lance finished the food in silence, rose stiffly and began to dress.

'Thanks for takin' care of me, Otto,' he told the lawman. 'Can you lend me a hat?'

'Why, sure,' replied the Marshal, reaching for a spare piece of headgear on a hook. 'Where you goin'?'

'Out to Spring River. Where's my gelding?'

'Down at the livery-stable,' Gantz replied.

'Lance, you ain't ridin' to Spring River now,' put in Zeb Dockery. 'It's snowing right furious an' you ain't in good shape!'

'I'm goin' just the same,' retorted Lance, easing himself into his slicker. He headed for the door on legs still slightly unsteady.

'Thanks for everythin', boys,' he called before going out into the wind-driven whiteness.

He rode steadily out of town, the snowflakes feathering wetly against his face.

The days of the Sioux were over, he thought, and these last months had been unhappy ones for the once-proud people of the plains. But there was one to whom he was going to give all the happiness in his power.

She had kissed him once, in the white swirl of a snow storm, and now he was riding out to Spring River to take her in his arms and feel the snow-wet softness of her face against his own once again. The gloomy days of winter would be followed by the warmth of spring, bringing a promise of happiness for white and Indian alike.

And Eloise Sun-on-Water would be his very own.

THE END

We do hope that you have enjoyed reading this large print book.

Did you know that all of our titles are available for purchase?

We publish a wide range of high quality large print books including:
Romances, Mysteries, Classics
General Fiction
Non Fiction and Westerns

Special interest titles available in large print are:
The Little Oxford Dictionary
Music Book, Song Book
Hymn Book, Service Book

Also available from us courtesy of Oxford University Press:
Young Readers' Dictionary
(large print edition)
Young Readers' Thesaurus
(large print edition)

For further information or a free brochure, please contact us at:
Ulverscroft Large Print Books Ltd.,
The Green, Bradgate Road, Anstey,
Leicester, LE7 7FU, England.
Tel: (00 44) **0116 236 4325**
Fax: (00 44) **0116 234 0205**

RODEO RENEGADE

Ty Kirwan

When English couple Rufus and Nancy Medford inherit a ranch in New Mexico, they find the majority of their neighbours are hostile to strangers. Befriended by only one rancher, and plagued by rustlers, the thought of returning to England is tempting, but needing to prove himself, Rufus is coached as a fighter by a circus sharp shooter, the mysterious Ghost of the Cimarron. But will this be enough to overcome the frightening odds against him?

CABEL

Paul K. McAfee

Josh Cabel returned home from the Civil War to find his family all murdered by rioting members of Quantrill's band. The hunt for the killers led Josh to Colorado City where, after months of searching, he finally settled down to work on a ranch nearby. He saved the life of an Indian, who led him to a cache of weapons waiting for Sitting Bull's attack on the Whites. His involvement threw Cabel into grave danger. When the final confrontation came, who had the fastest — and deadlier — draw?

RIVERBOAT

Alan C. Porter

When Rufus Blake died he was found to be carrying a gold bar from a Confederate gold shipment that had disappeared twenty years before. This inspires Wes Hardiman and Ben Travis to swap horse and trail for a riverboat, the *River Queen*, on the Mississippi, in an effort to find the missing gold. Cord Duval is set on destroying the *River Queen* and he has the power and the gunmen to do it. Guns blaze as Hardiman and Travis attempt to unravel the mystery and stay alive.

MCKINNEY'S LAW

Mike Stotter

McKinney didn't count on coming across a dead body in the middle of Texas. He was about to become involved in an ever-deepening mystery. The renegade Comanche warrior, Black Eagle, was on the loose, creating havoc; he didn't appear in McKinney's plans at all, not until the Comanche forced himself into his life. The US Army gave McKinney some relief to his problems, but it also added to them, and with two old friends McKinney set about bringing justice through his own law.

BLACK RIVER

Adam Wright

John Dyer has come to the insignificant little town of Black River to destroy the last living reminder of his dark past. He has come to kill. Jack Hart is determined to stop him. Only he knows the terrible truth that has driven Dyer here, and he knows that only he can beat Dyer in a gunfight. Ex-lawman Brad Harris is after Dyer too — to avenge his family. The stage is set for madness, death and vengeance.